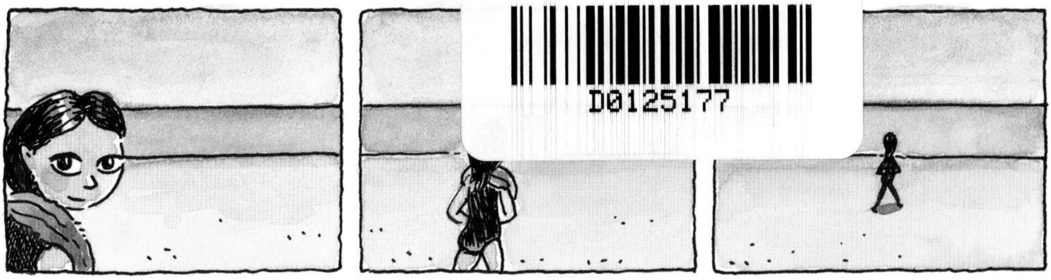

to dance

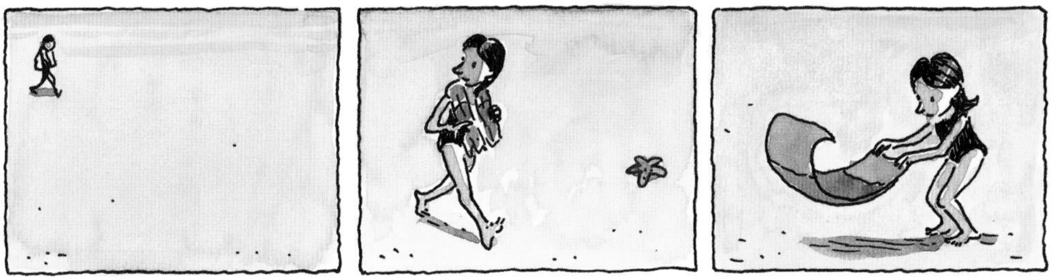

a memoir by Siena Cherson Siegel

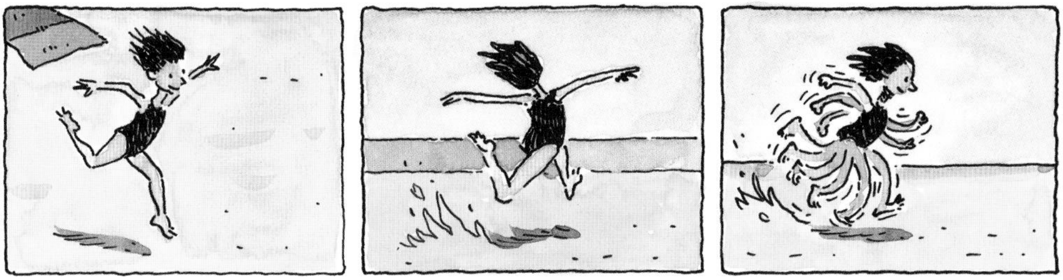

with artwork by Mark Siegel

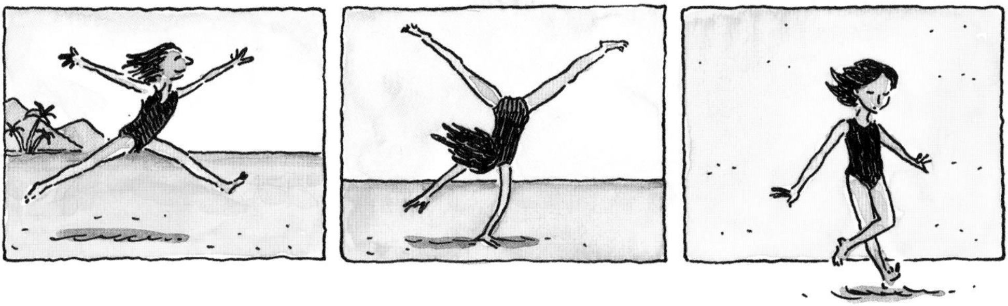

Aladdin Paperbacks New York London Toronto Sydney

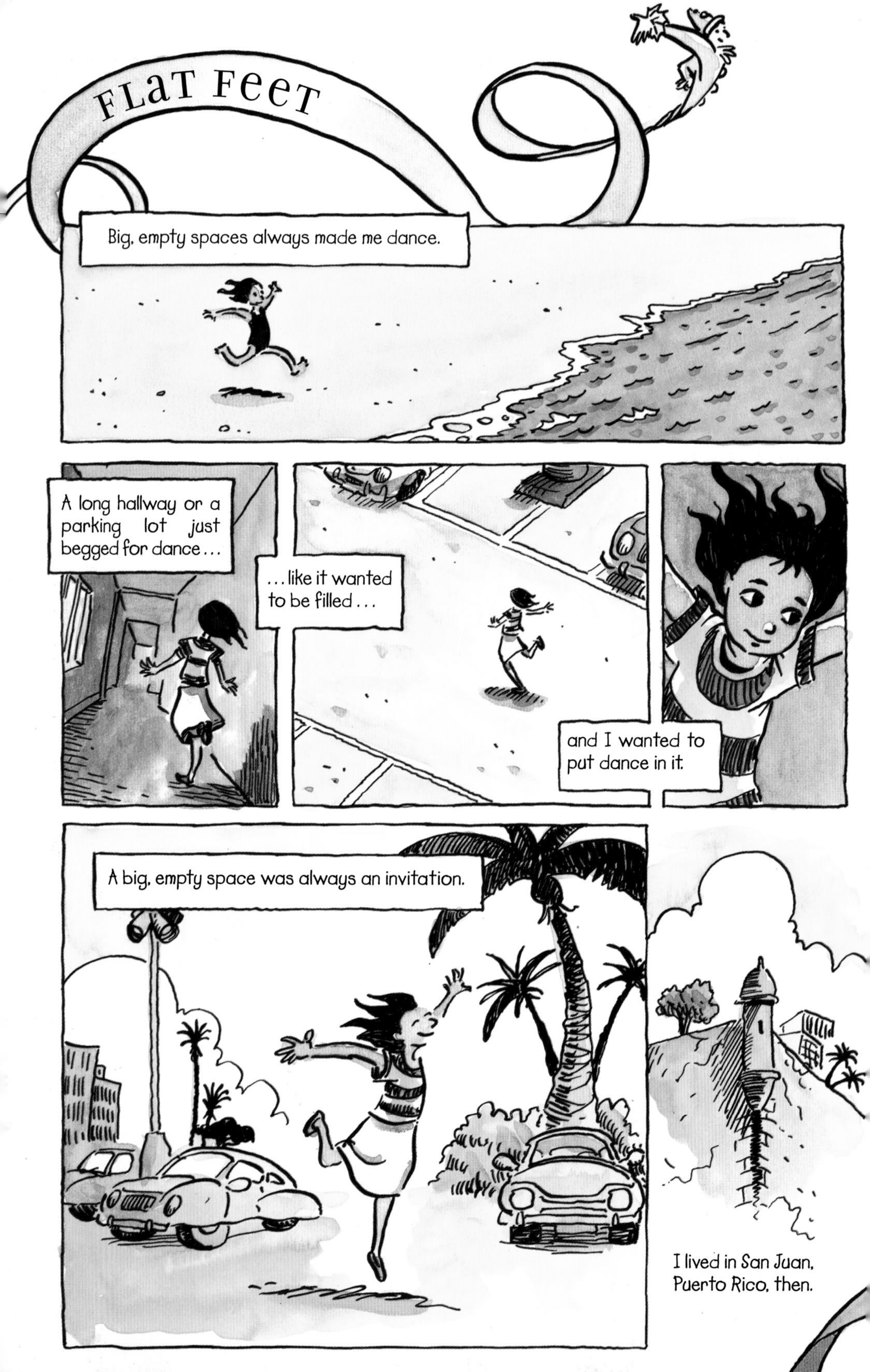

Flat Feet
Big, empty spaces always made me dance.
A long hallway or a parking lot just begged for dance...
...like it wanted to be filled...
and I wanted to put dance in it.
A big, empty space was always an invitation.
I lived in San Juan, Puerto Rico, then.

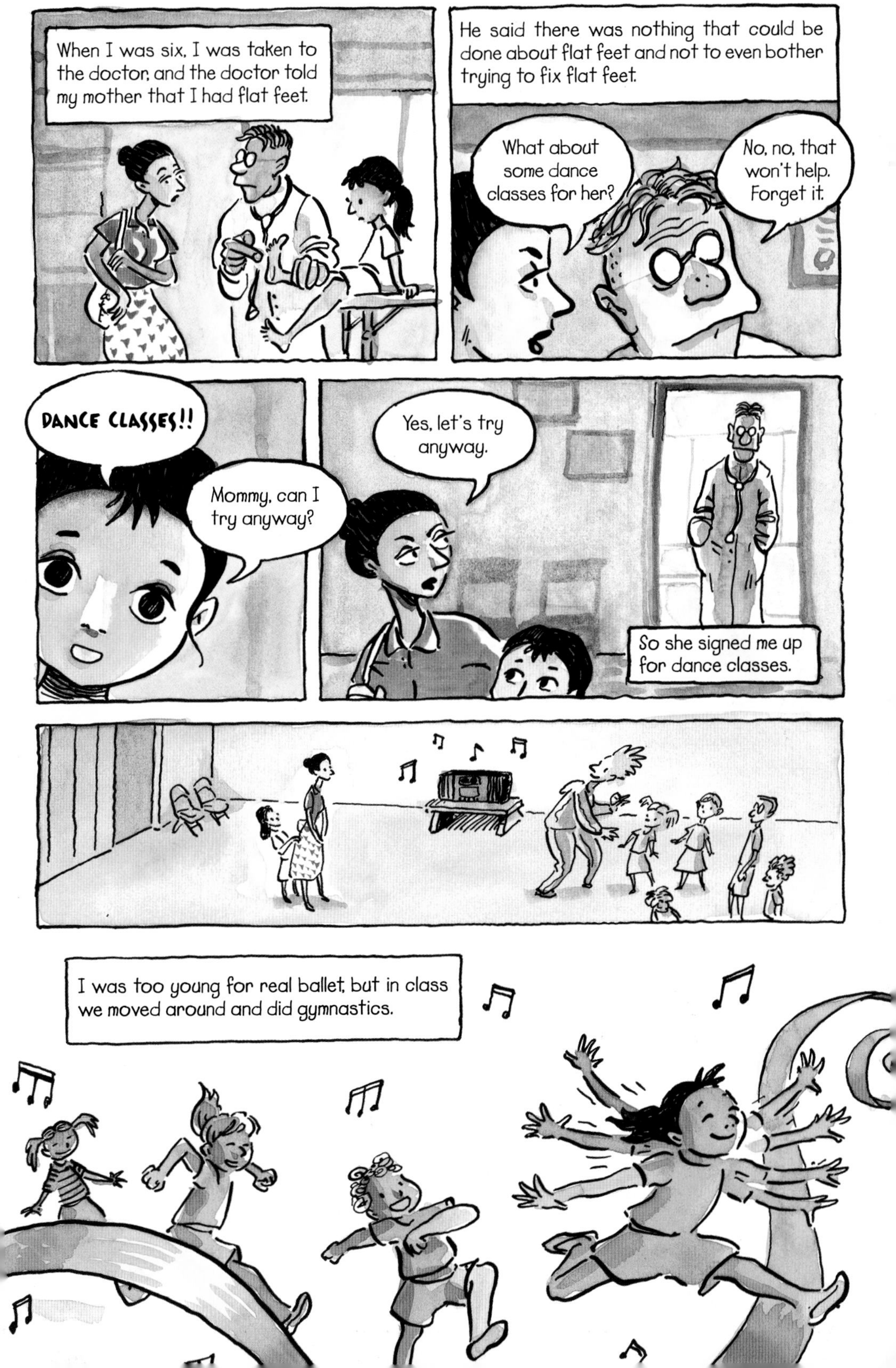
When I was six, I was taken to the doctor, and the doctor told my mother that I had flat feet.
He said there was nothing that could be done about flat feet and not to even bother trying to fix flat feet.
What about some dance classes for her?
No, no, that won't help. Forget it.
DANCE CLASSES!!
Mommy, can I try anyway?
Yes, let's try anyway.
So she signed me up for dance classes.
I was too young for real ballet, but in class we moved around and did gymnastics.

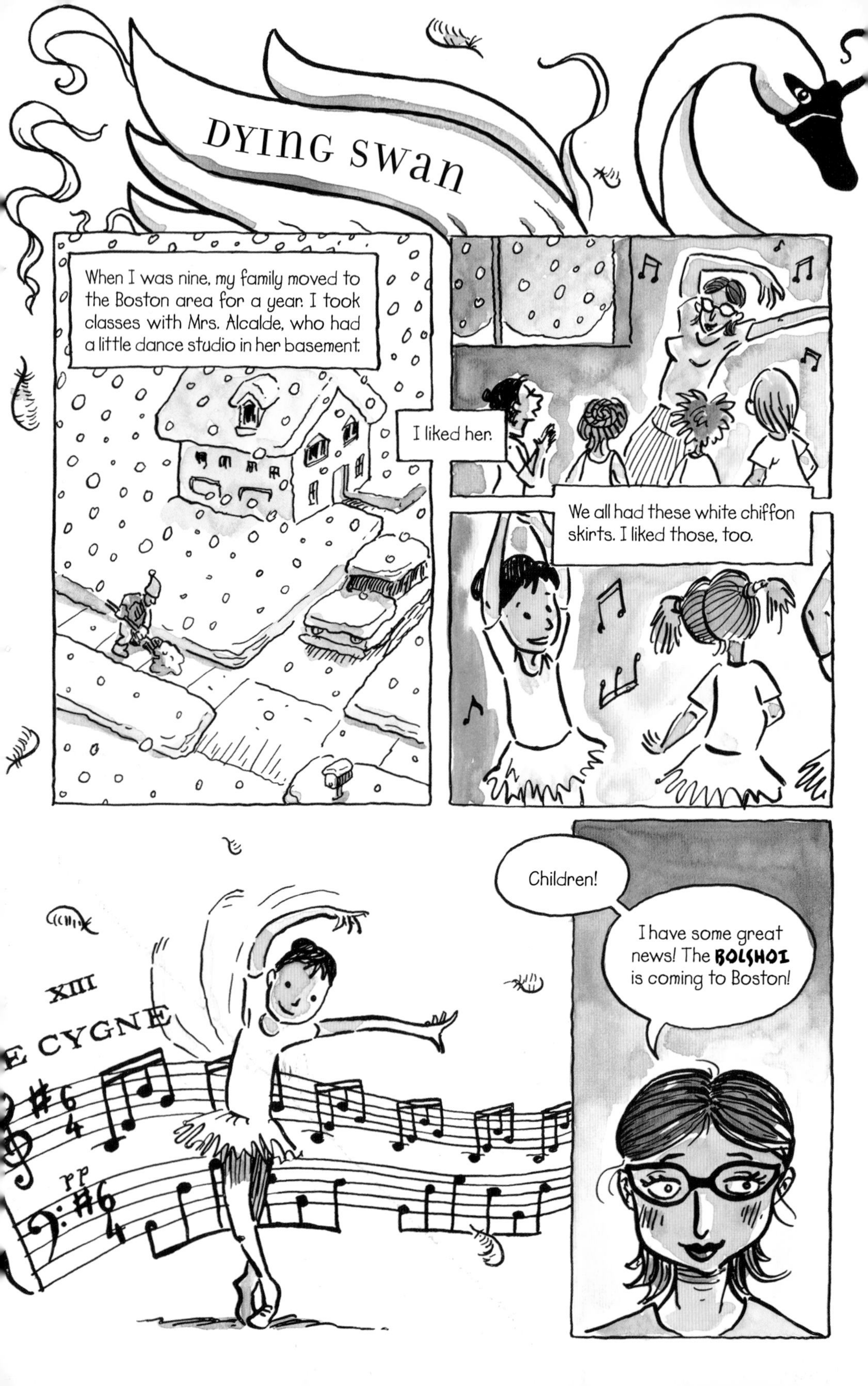
DYING SWAN
When I was nine, my family moved to the Boston area for a year. I took classes with Mrs. Alcalde, who had a little dance studio in her basement.
I liked her.
We all had these white chiffon skirts. I liked those, too.
XIII
E CYGNE
pp
Children!
I have some great news! The BOLSHOI is coming to Boston!

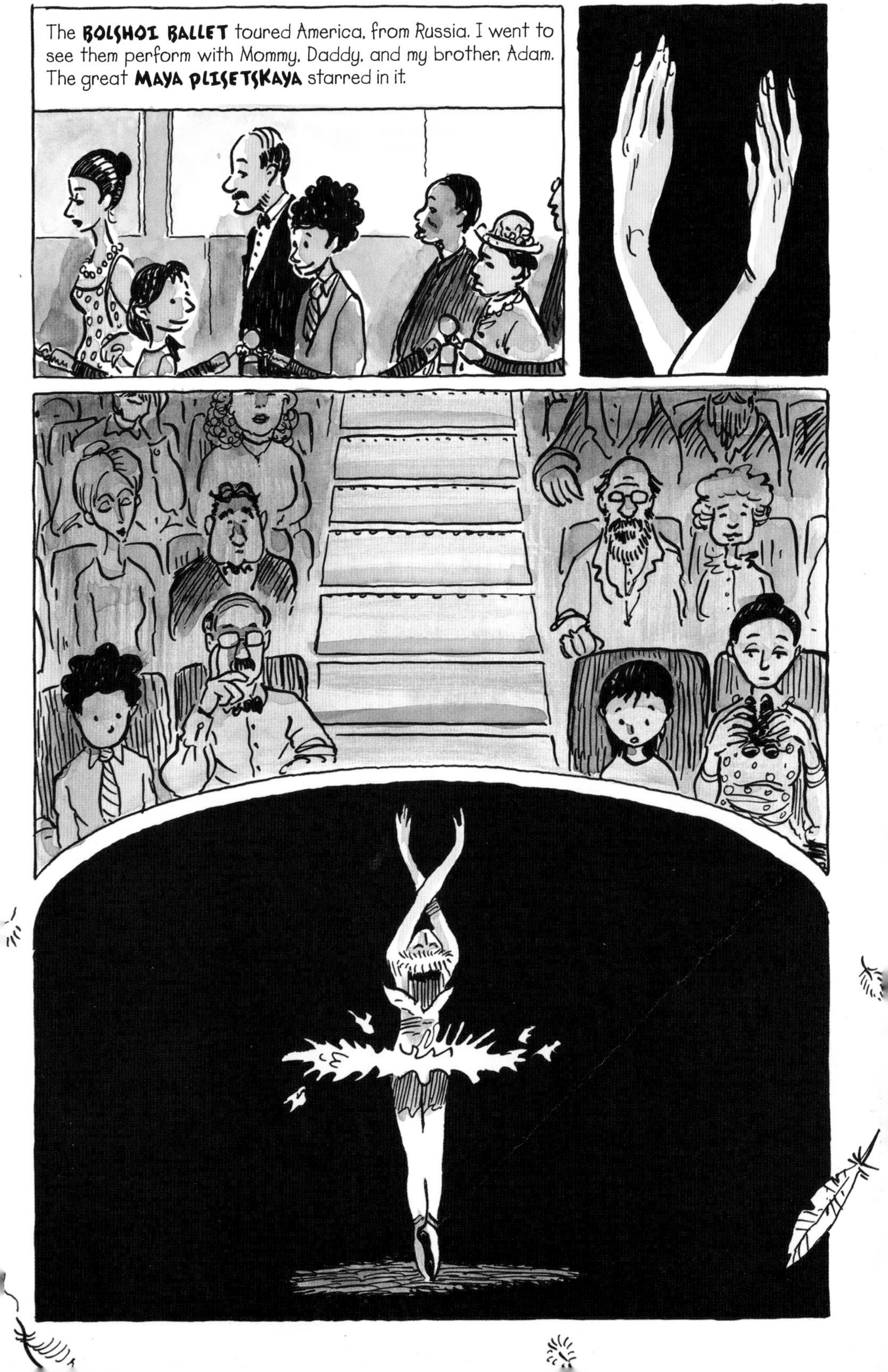
The BOLSHOI BALLET toured America, from Russia. I went to see them perform with Mommy, Daddy, and my brother, Adam. The great MAYA PLISETSKAYA starred in it.

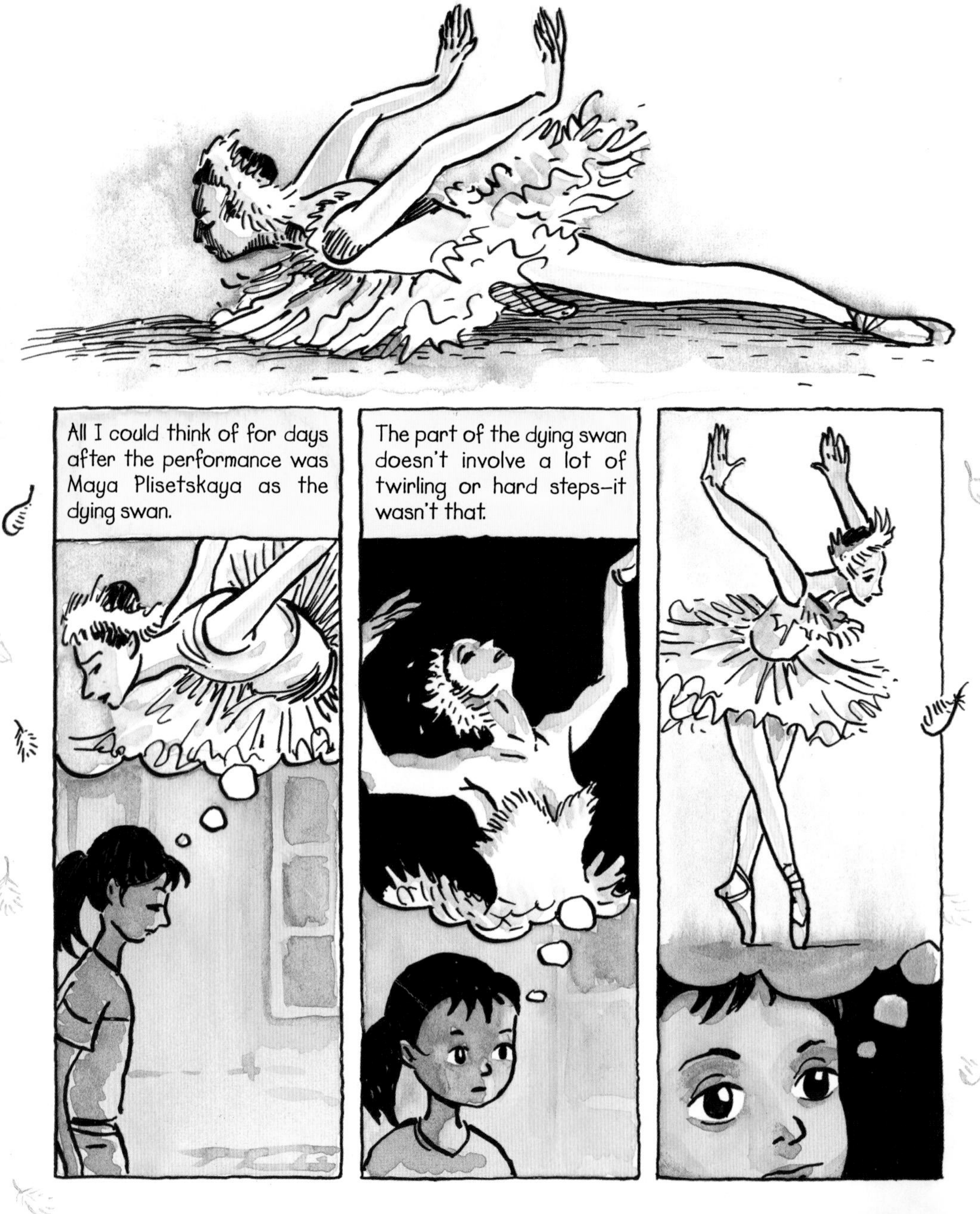
All I could think of for days after the performance was Maya Plisetskaya as the dying swan.
The part of the dying swan doesn't involve a lot of twirling or hard steps—it wasn't that.

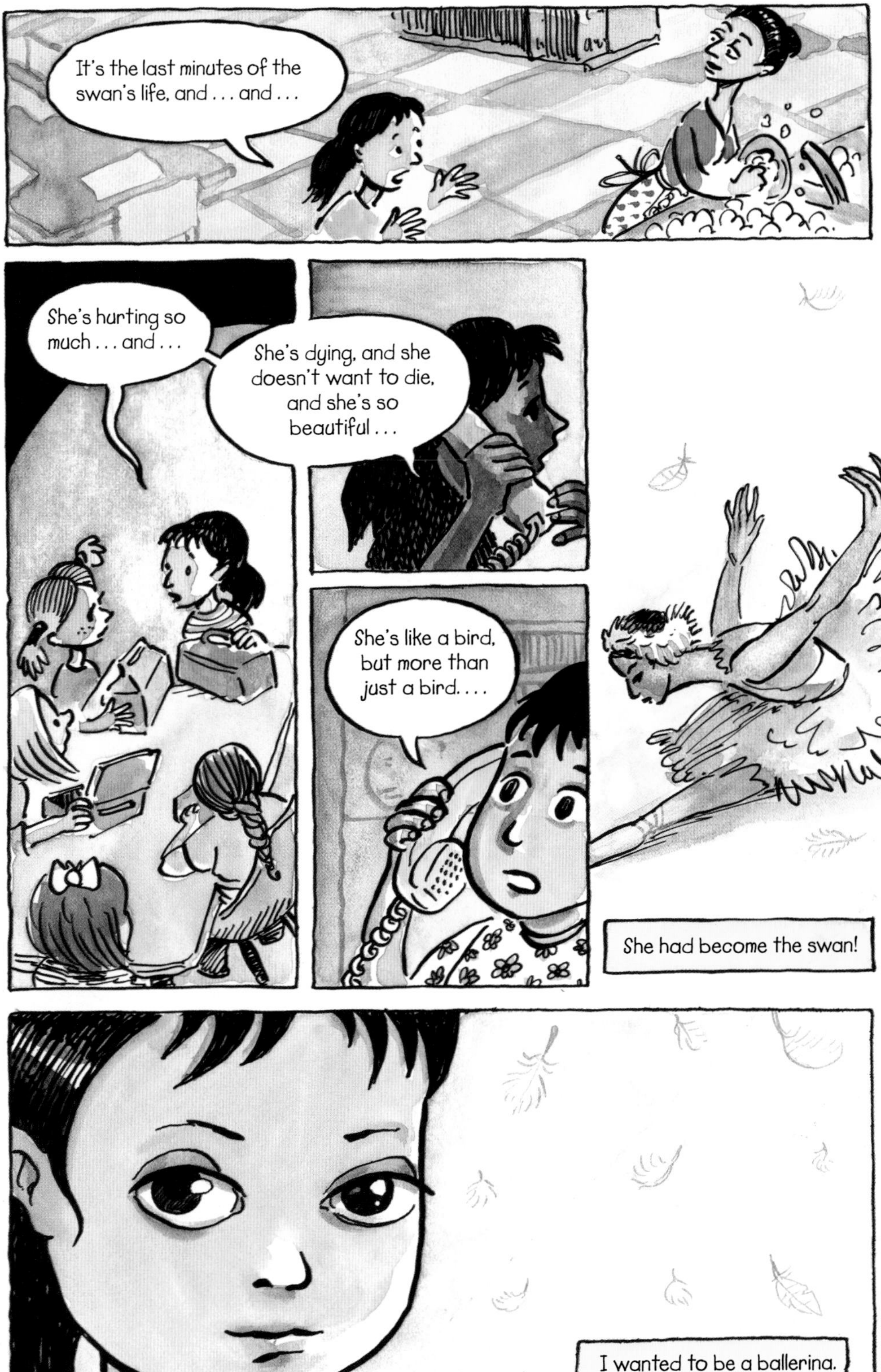
It's the last minutes of the swan's life, and . . . and . . .
She's hurting so much . . . and . . .
She's dying, and she doesn't want to die, and she's so beautiful . . .
She's like a bird, but more than just a bird. . . .
She had become the swan!
I wanted to be a ballerina.

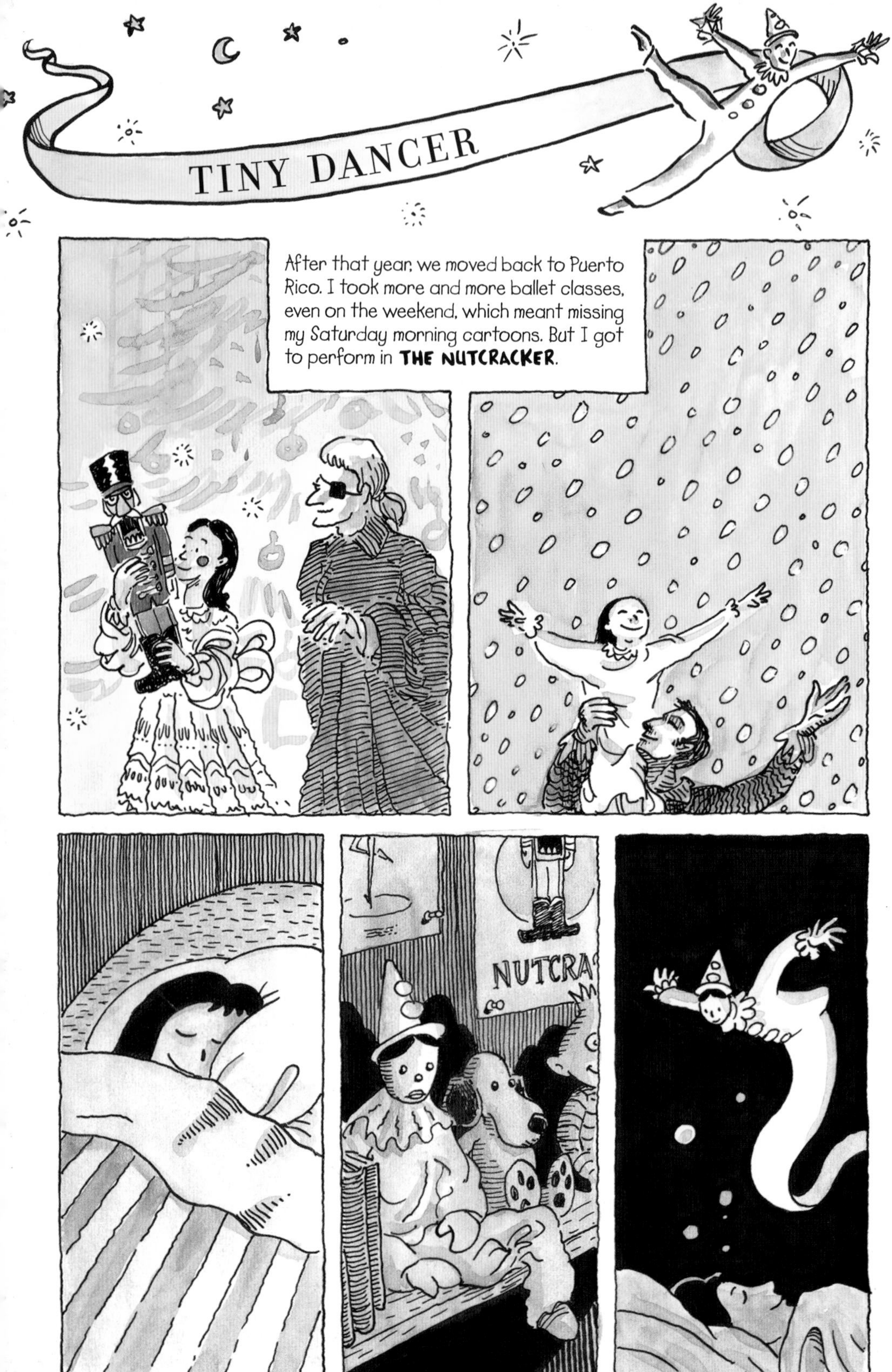
TINY DANCER
After that year, we moved back to Puerto Rico. I took more and more ballet classes, even on the weekend, which meant missing my Saturday morning cartoons. But I got to perform in THE NUTCRACKER.
NUTCRA

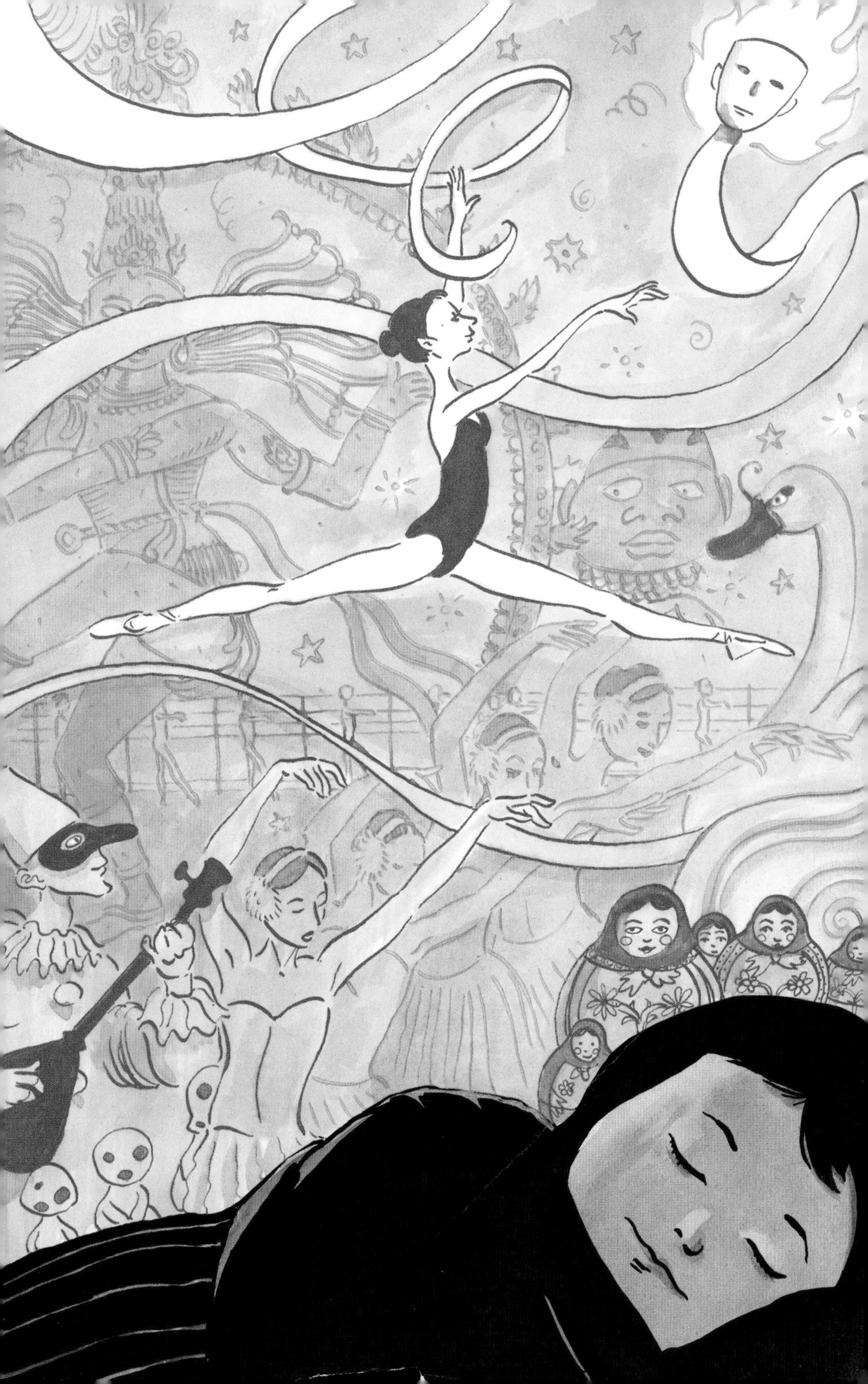

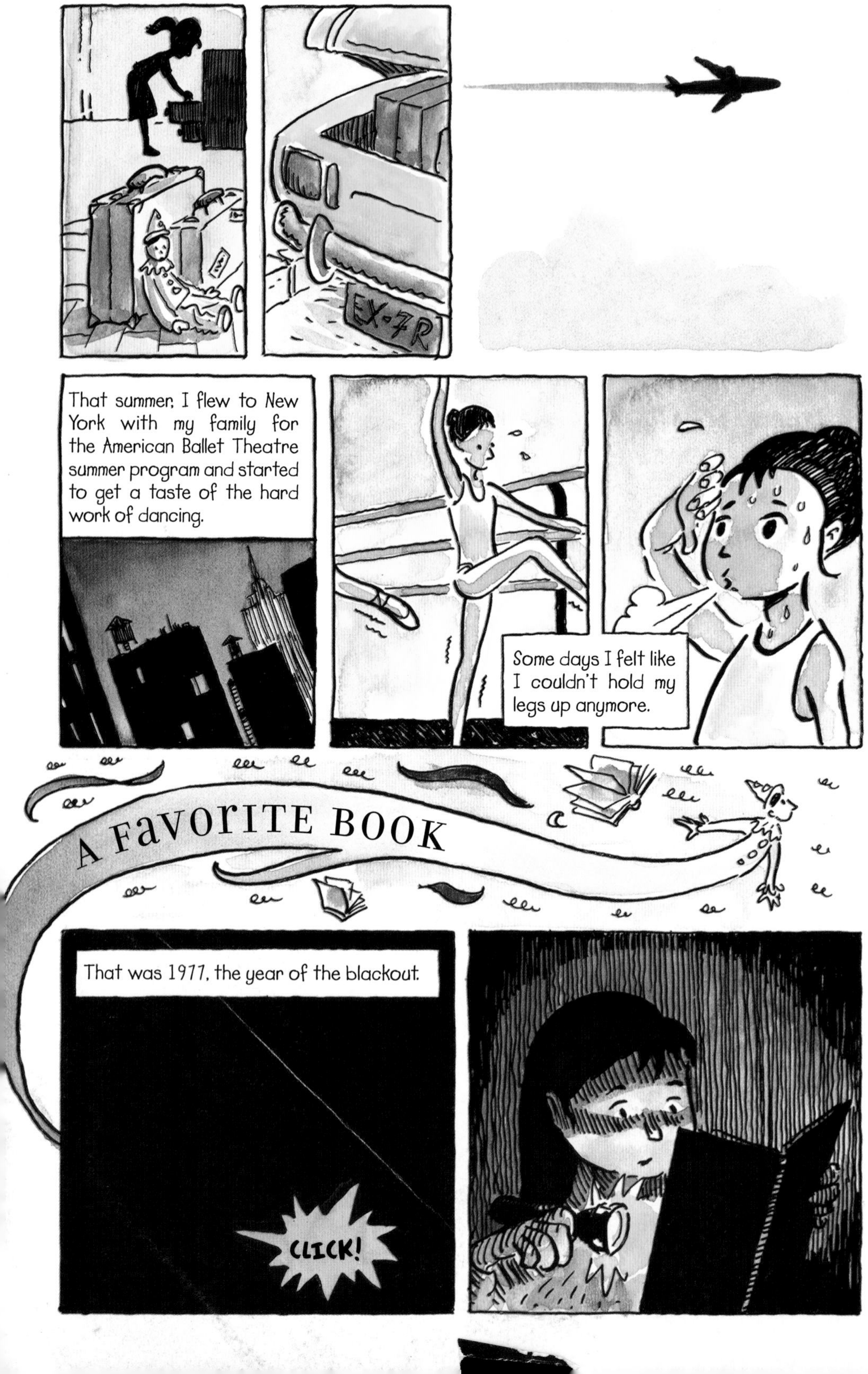
EX-7R
That summer, I flew to New York with my family for the American Ballet Theatre summer program and started to get a taste of the hard work of dancing.
Some days I felt like I couldn't hold my legs up anymore.
A FAVORITE BOOK
That was 1977, the year of the blackout.
CLICK!

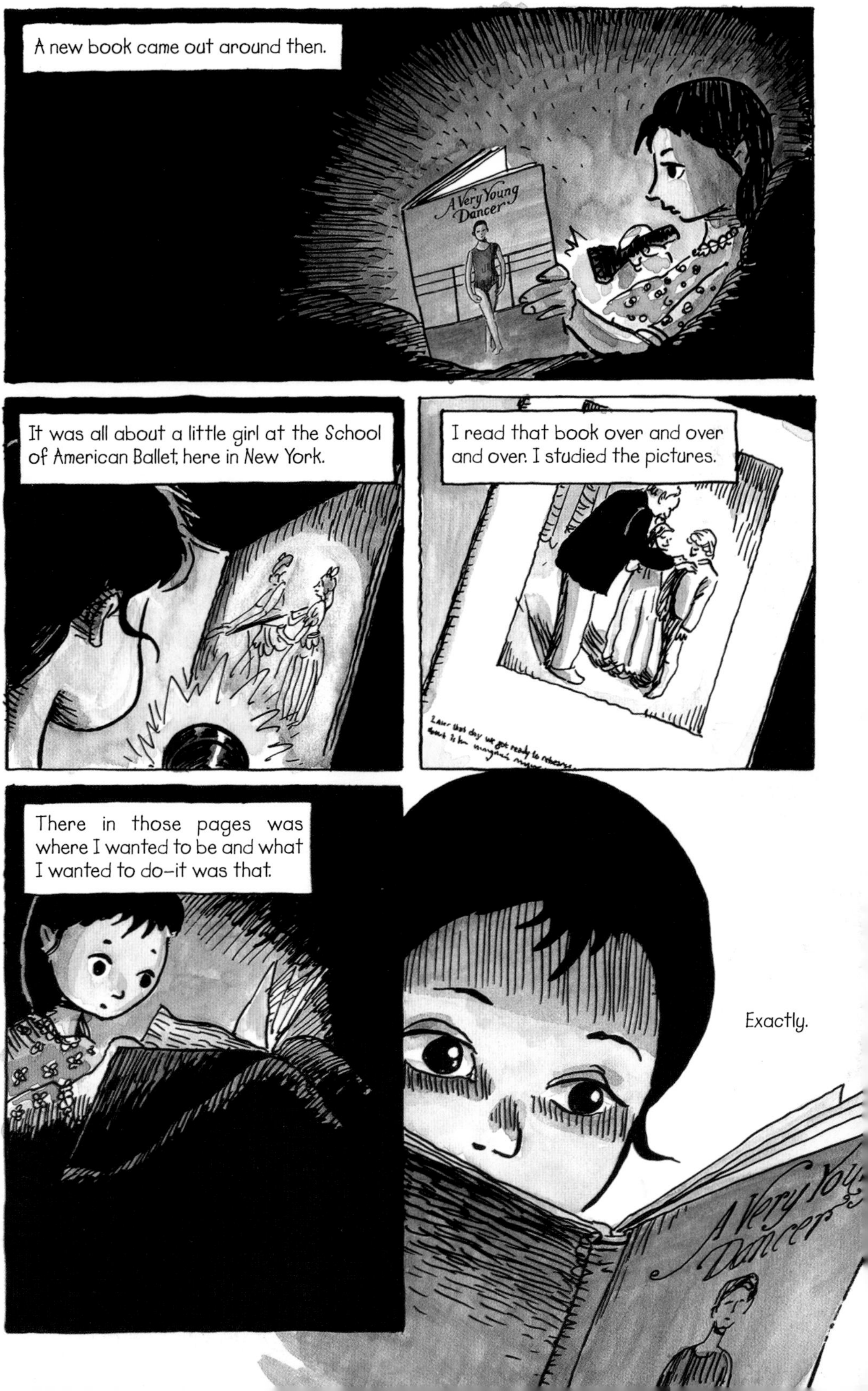
A new book came out around then.
A Very Young Dancer
It was all about a little girl at the School of American Ballet, here in New York.
I read that book over and over and over. I studied the pictures.
There in those pages was where I wanted to be and what I wanted to do—it was that.
Exactly.

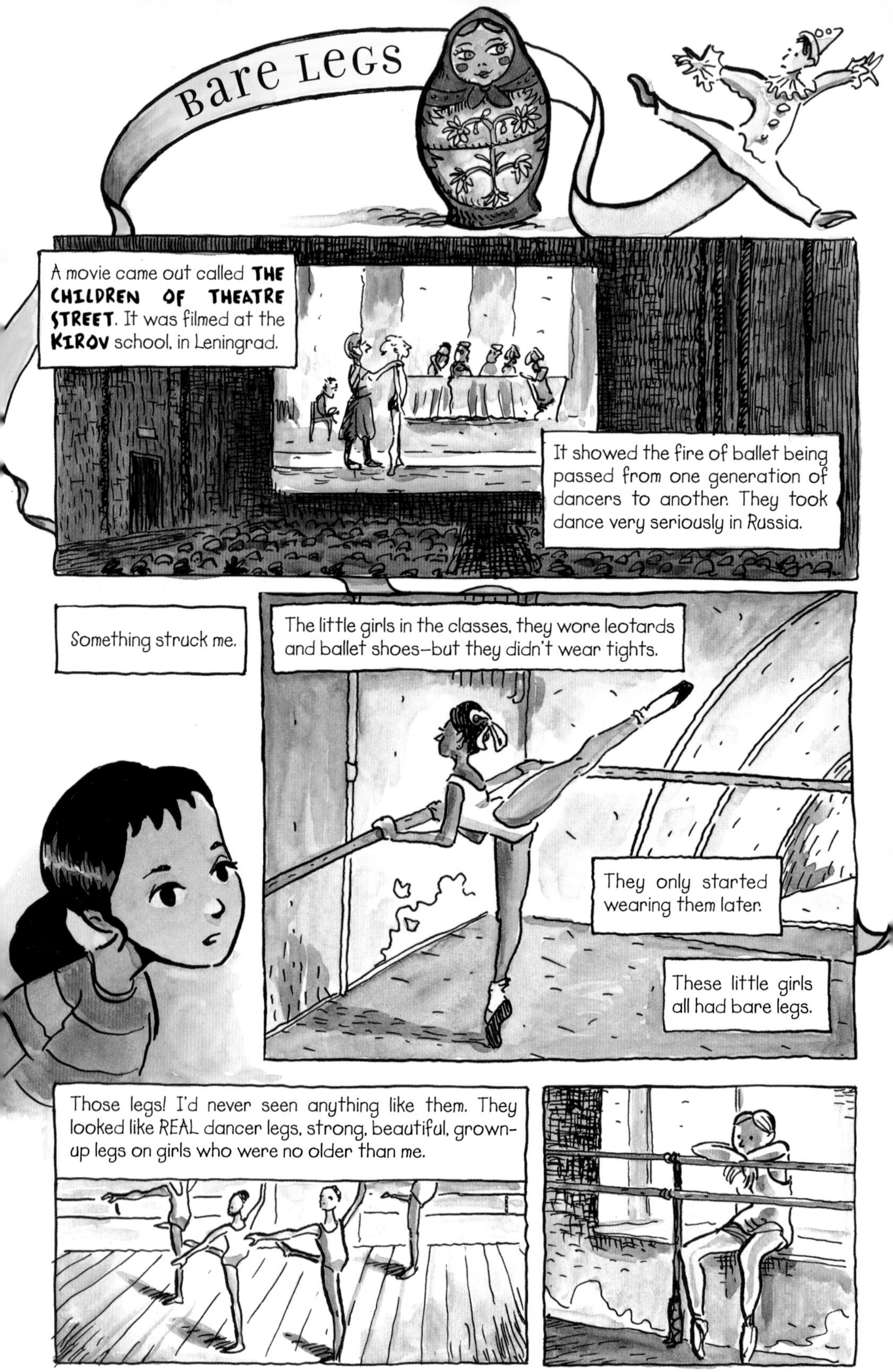
Bare Legs
A movie came out called THE CHILDREN OF THEATRE STREET. It was filmed at the KIROV school, in Leningrad.
It showed the fire of ballet being passed from one generation of dancers to another. They took dance very seriously in Russia.
Something struck me.
The little girls in the classes, they wore leotards and ballet shoes—but they didn't wear tights.
They only started wearing them later.
These little girls all had bare legs.
Those legs! I'd never seen anything like them. They looked like REAL dancer legs, strong, beautiful, grown-up legs on girls who were no older than me.

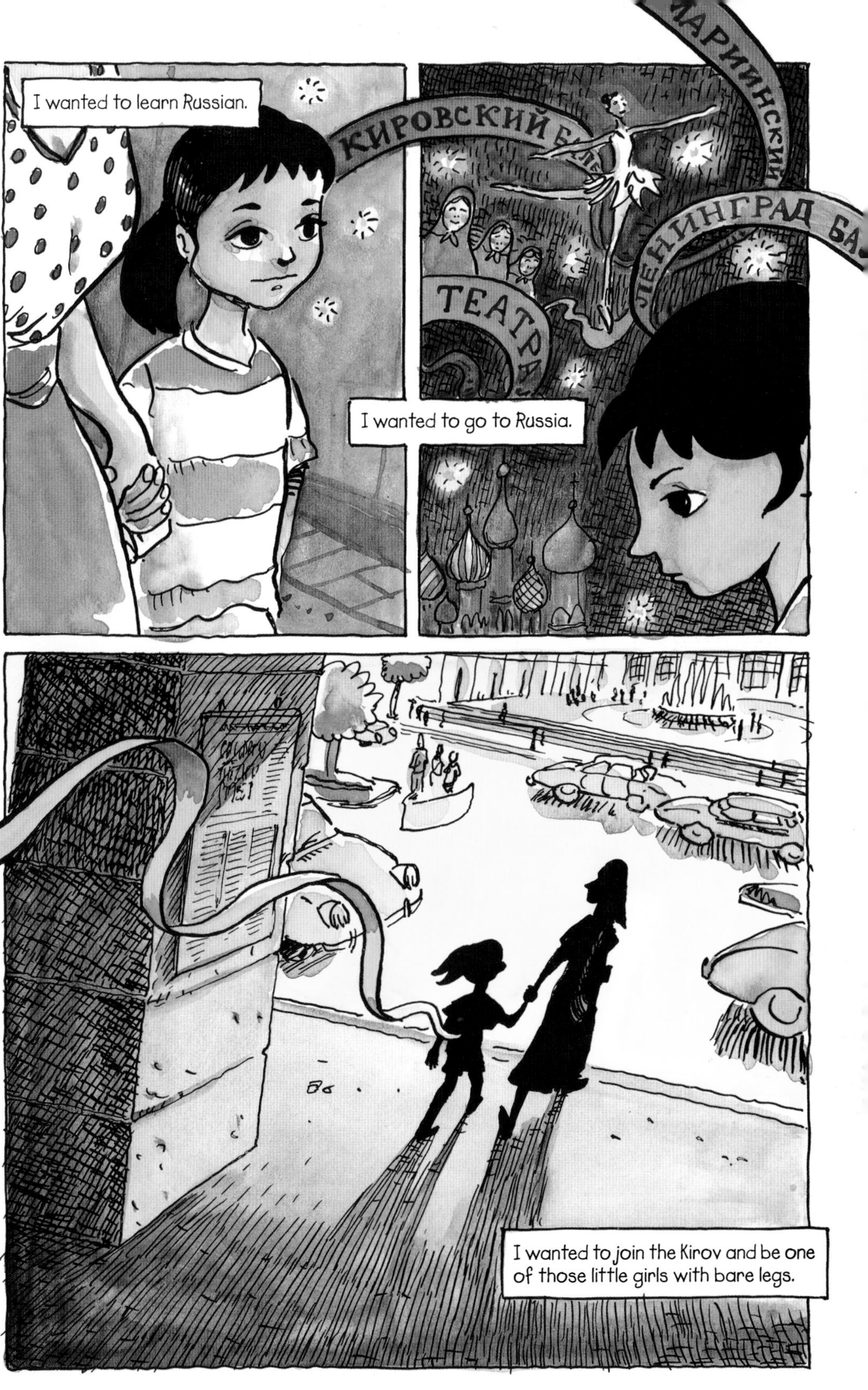
I wanted to learn Russian.
КИРОВСКИЙ
МАРИИНСКИЙ
ЛЕНИНГРАД
ТЕАТР
I wanted to go to Russia.
I wanted to join the Kirov and be one of those little girls with bare legs.

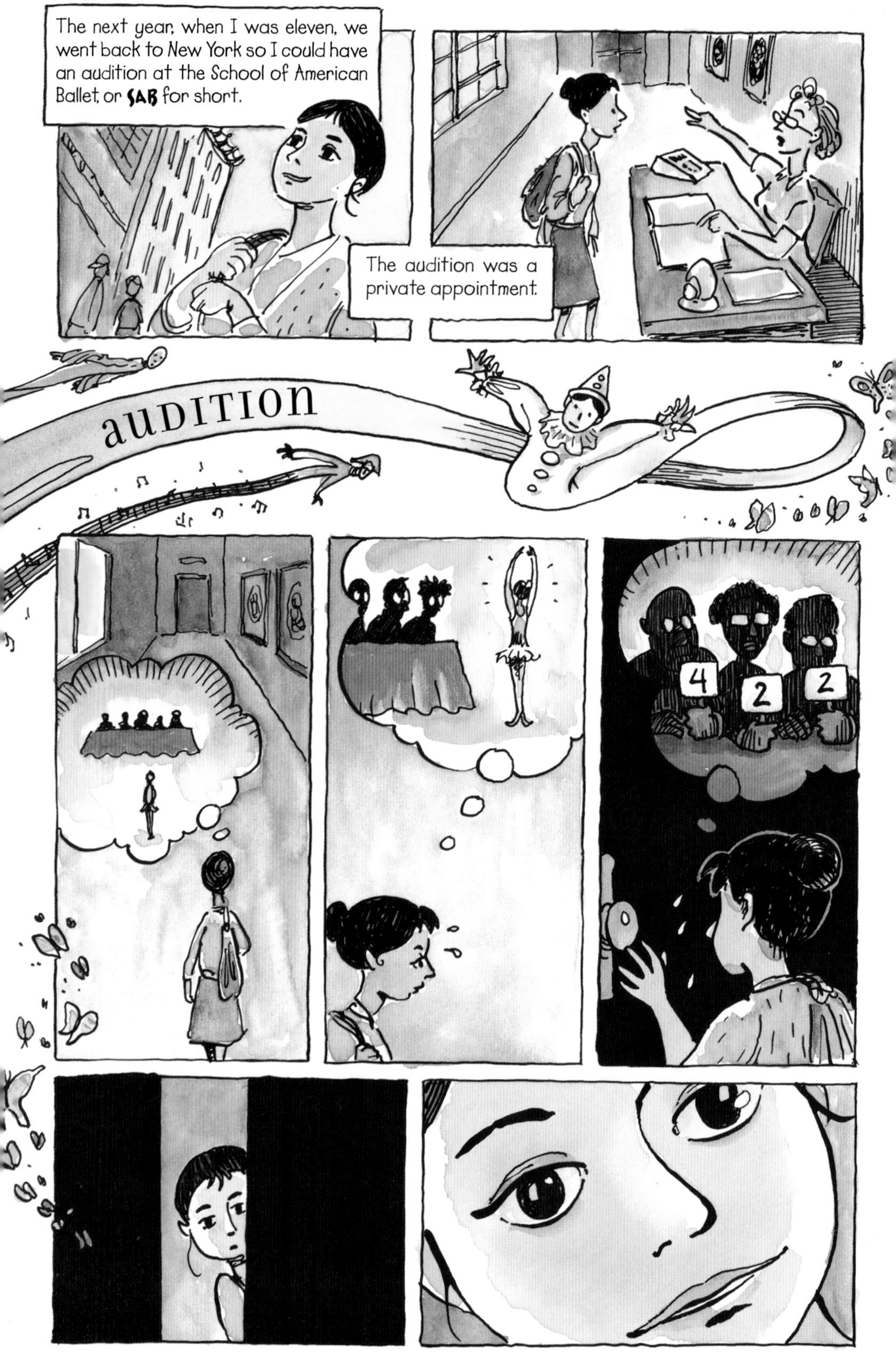
The next year, when I was eleven, we went back to New York so I could have an audition at the School of American Ballet, or SAB for short.
The audition was a private appointment.
audition
4
2
2

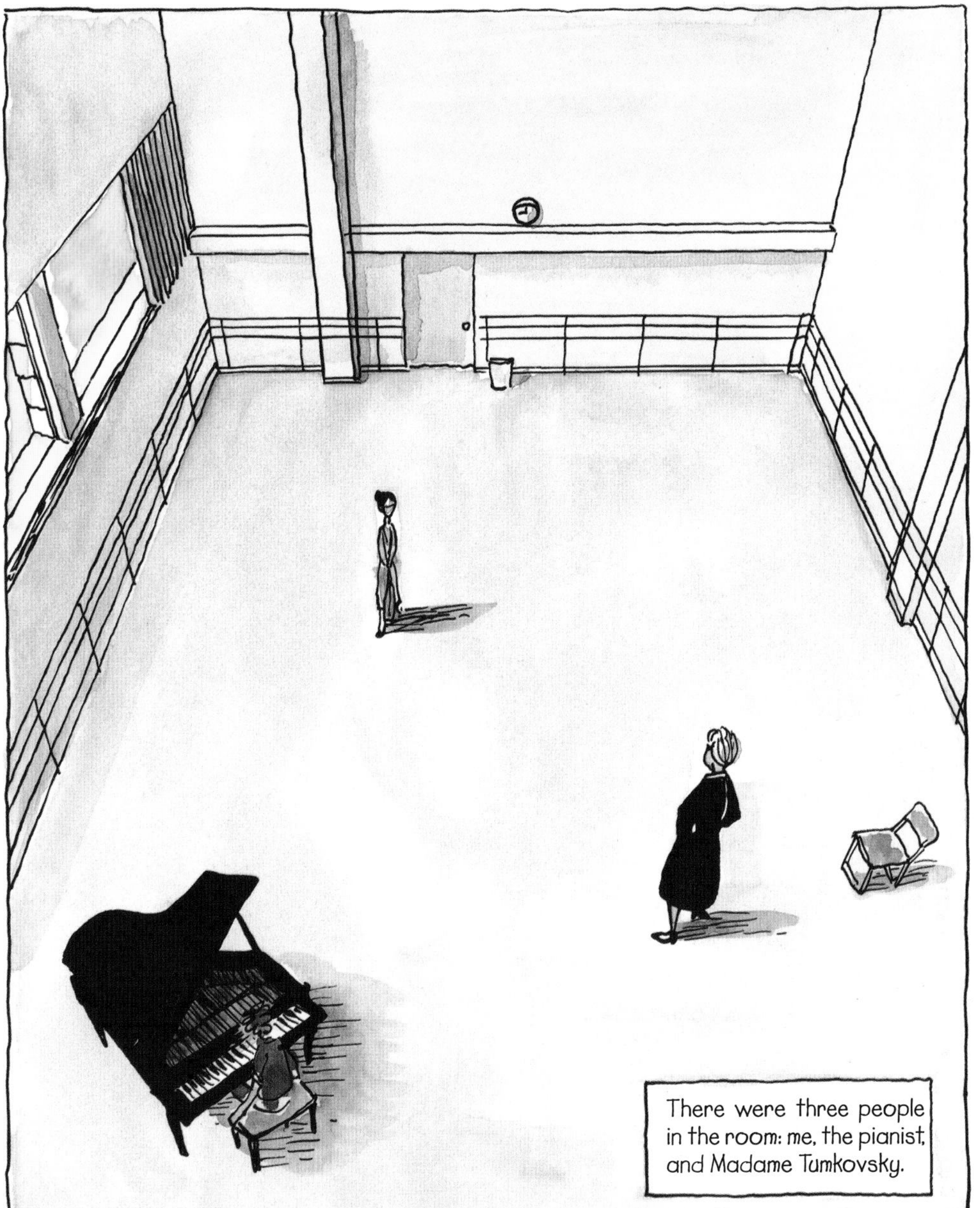
There were three people in the room: me, the pianist, and Madame Tumkovsky.

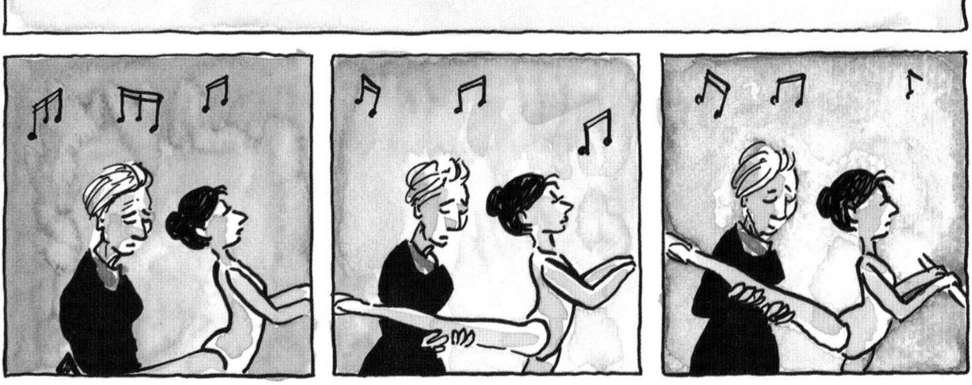

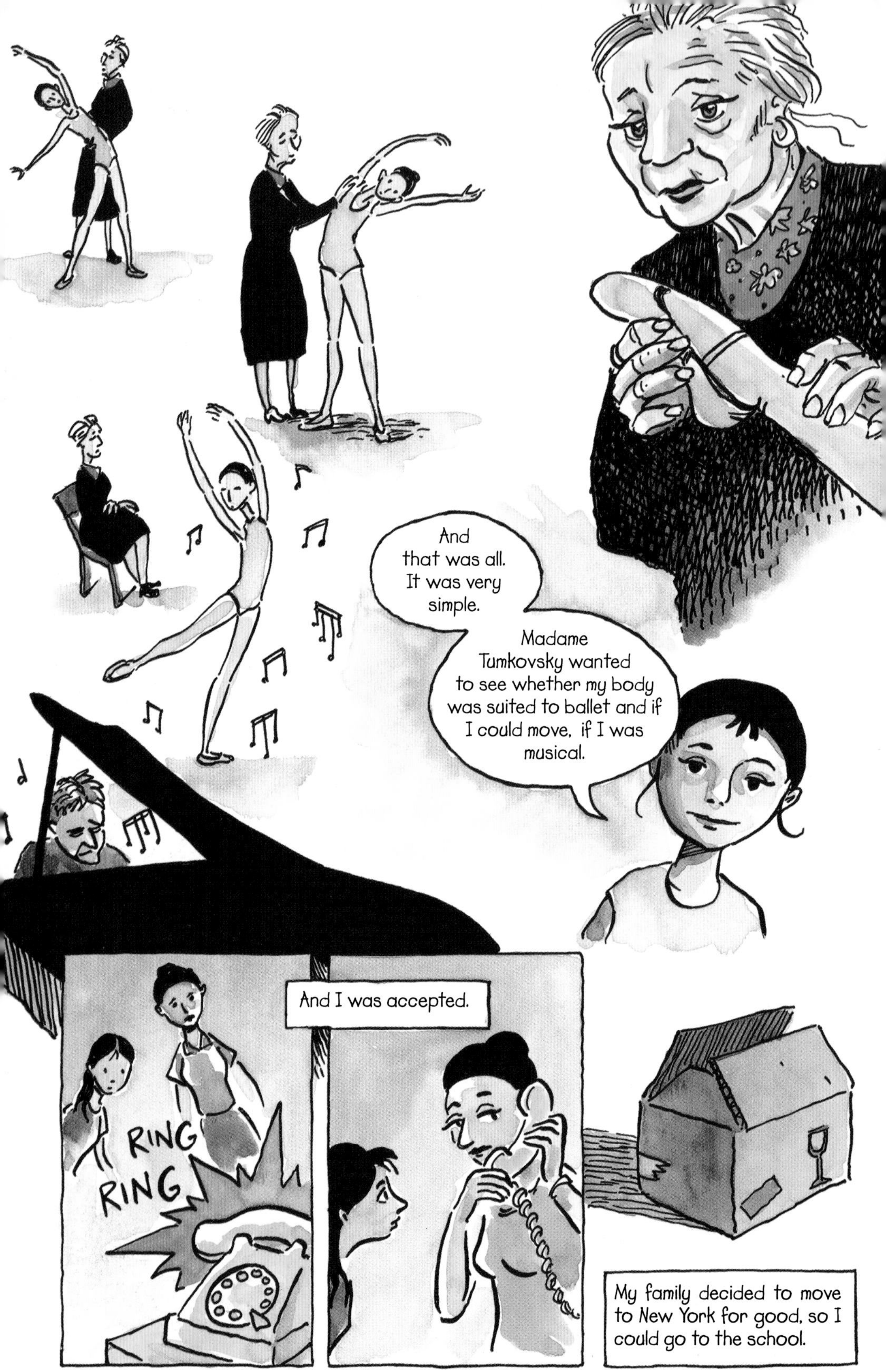
And that was all. It was very simple.
Madame Tumkovsky wanted to see whether my body was suited to ballet and if I could move, if I was musical.
And I was accepted.
RING RING
My family decided to move to New York for good, so I could go to the school.

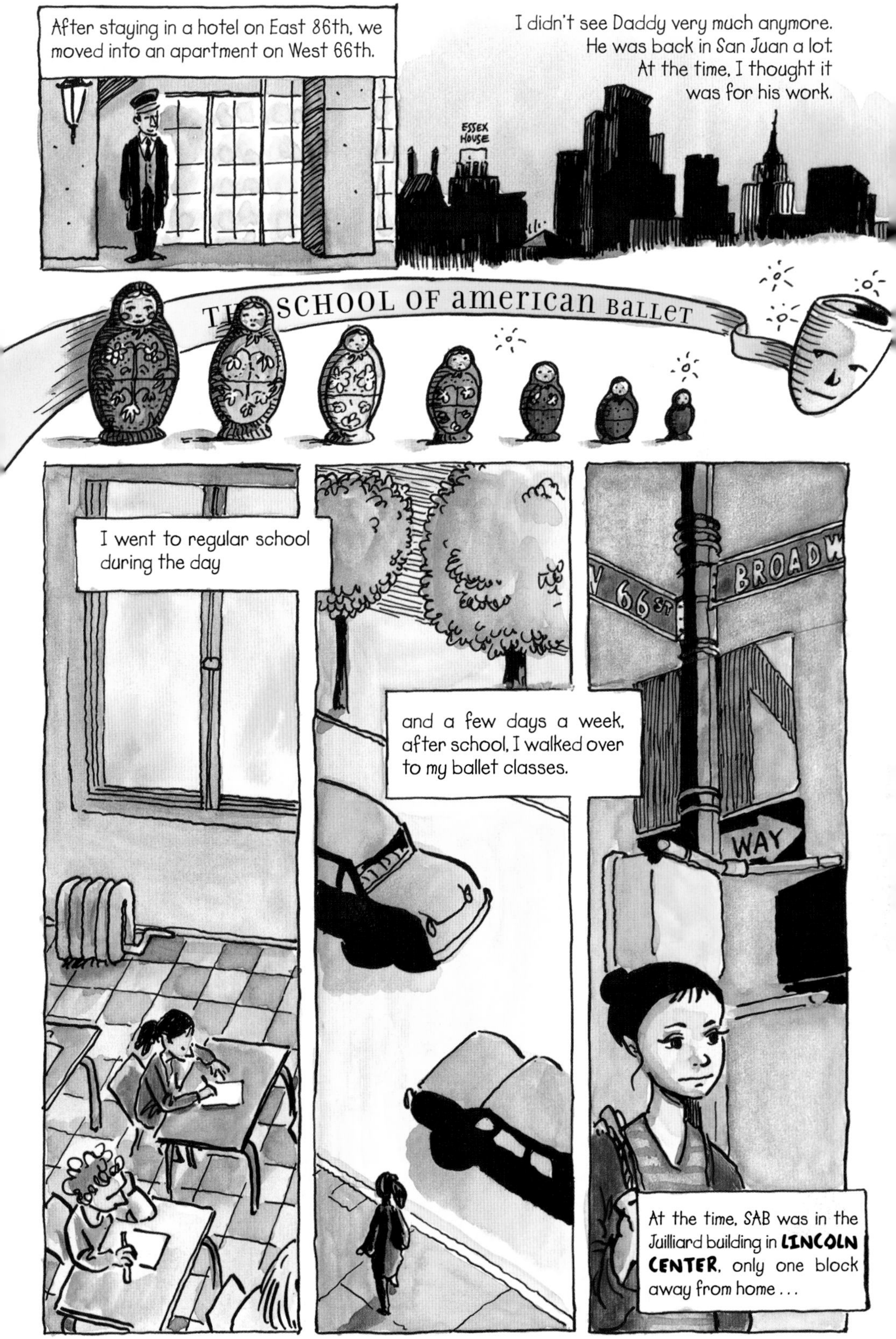

After staying in a hotel on East 86th, we moved into an apartment on West 66th.
I didn't see Daddy very much anymore. He was back in San Juan a lot. At the time, I thought it was for his work.
ESSEX HOUSE
SCHOOL OF american BaLLET
I went to regular school during the day
and a few days a week, after school, I walked over to my ballet classes.
66 ST
BROADW
WAY
At the time, SAB was in the Juilliard building in **LINCOLN CENTER**, only one block away from home . . .

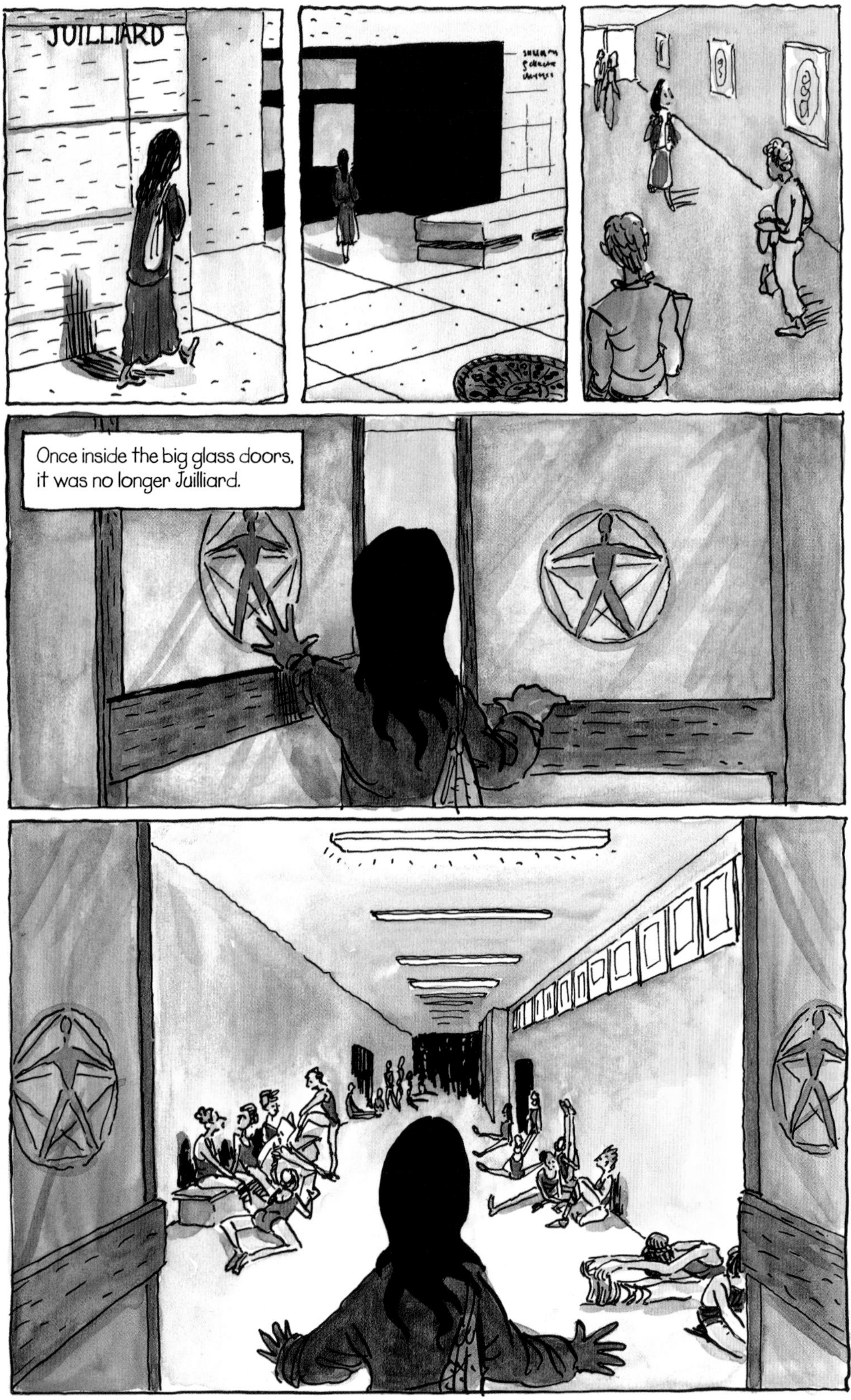
JUILLIARD
Once inside the big glass doors,
it was no longer Juilliard.

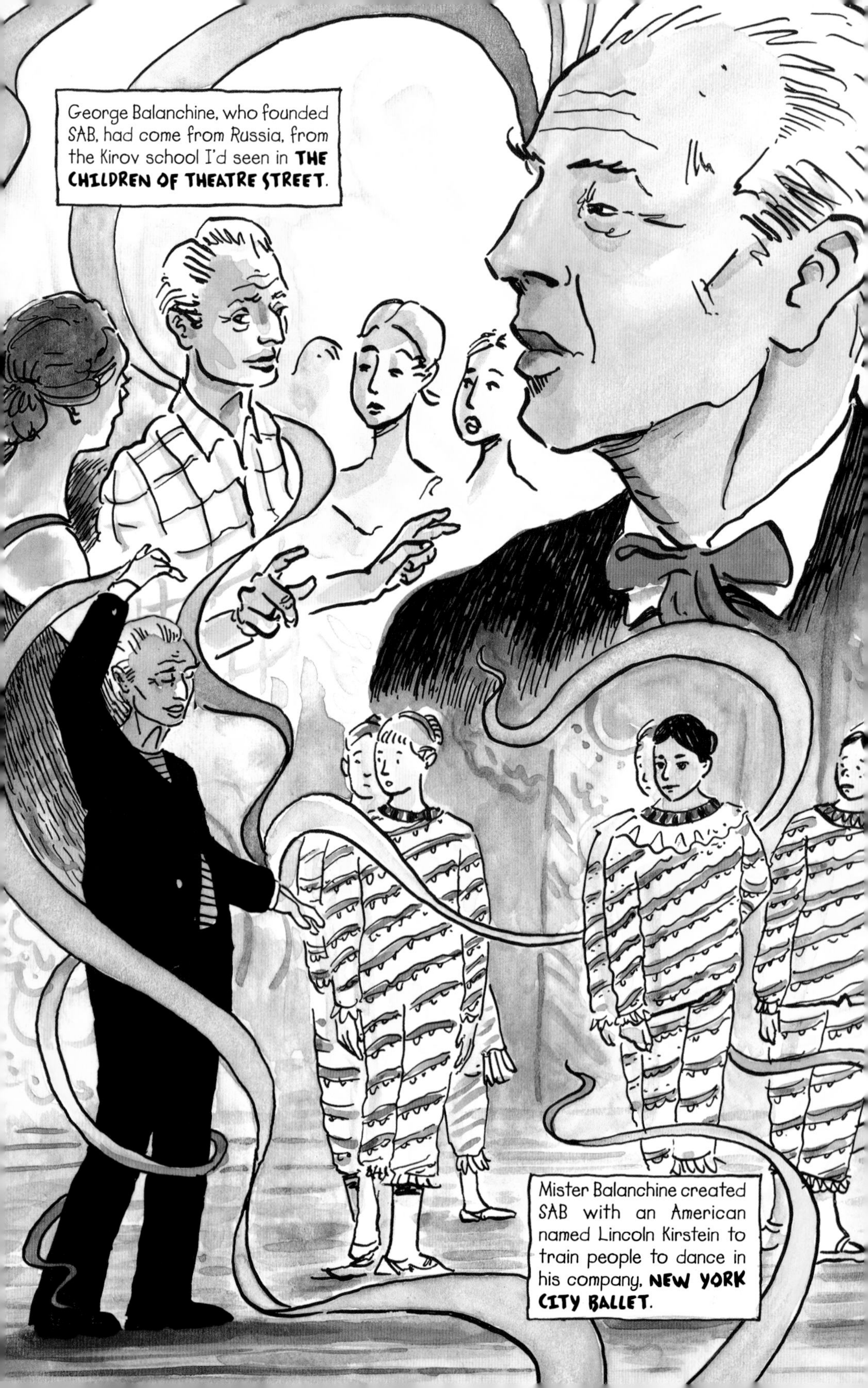
George Balanchine, who founded SAB, had come from Russia, from the Kirov school I'd seen in **THE CHILDREN OF THEATRE STREET**.
Mister Balanchine created SAB with an American named Lincoln Kirstein to train people to dance in his company, **NEW YORK CITY BALLET**.

MY FIRST TOE SHOES

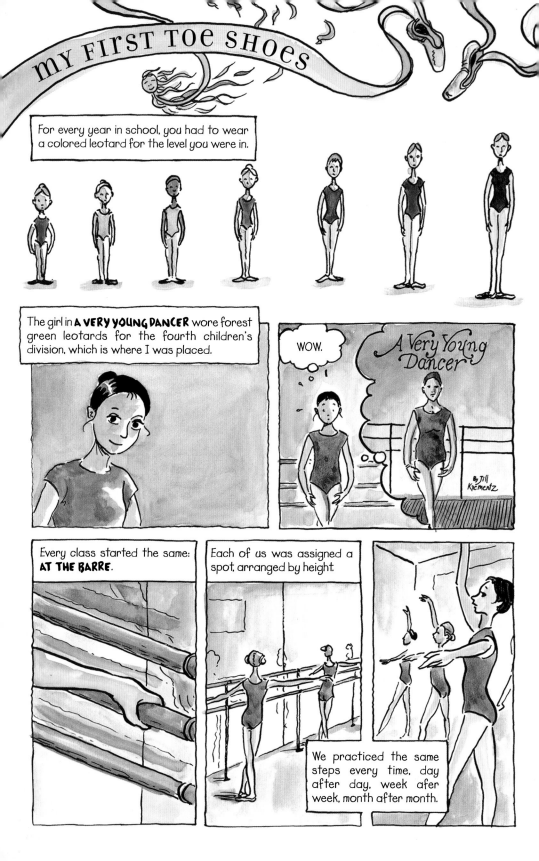

For every year in school, you had to wear a colored leotard for the level you were in.

The girl in **A VERY YOUNG DANCER** wore forest green leotards for the fourth children's division, which is where I was placed.

WOW.

A Very Young Dancer

By Jill Krementz

Every class started the same: **AT THE BARRE**.

Each of us was assigned a spot, arranged by height.

We practiced the same steps every time, day after day, week afer week, month after month.

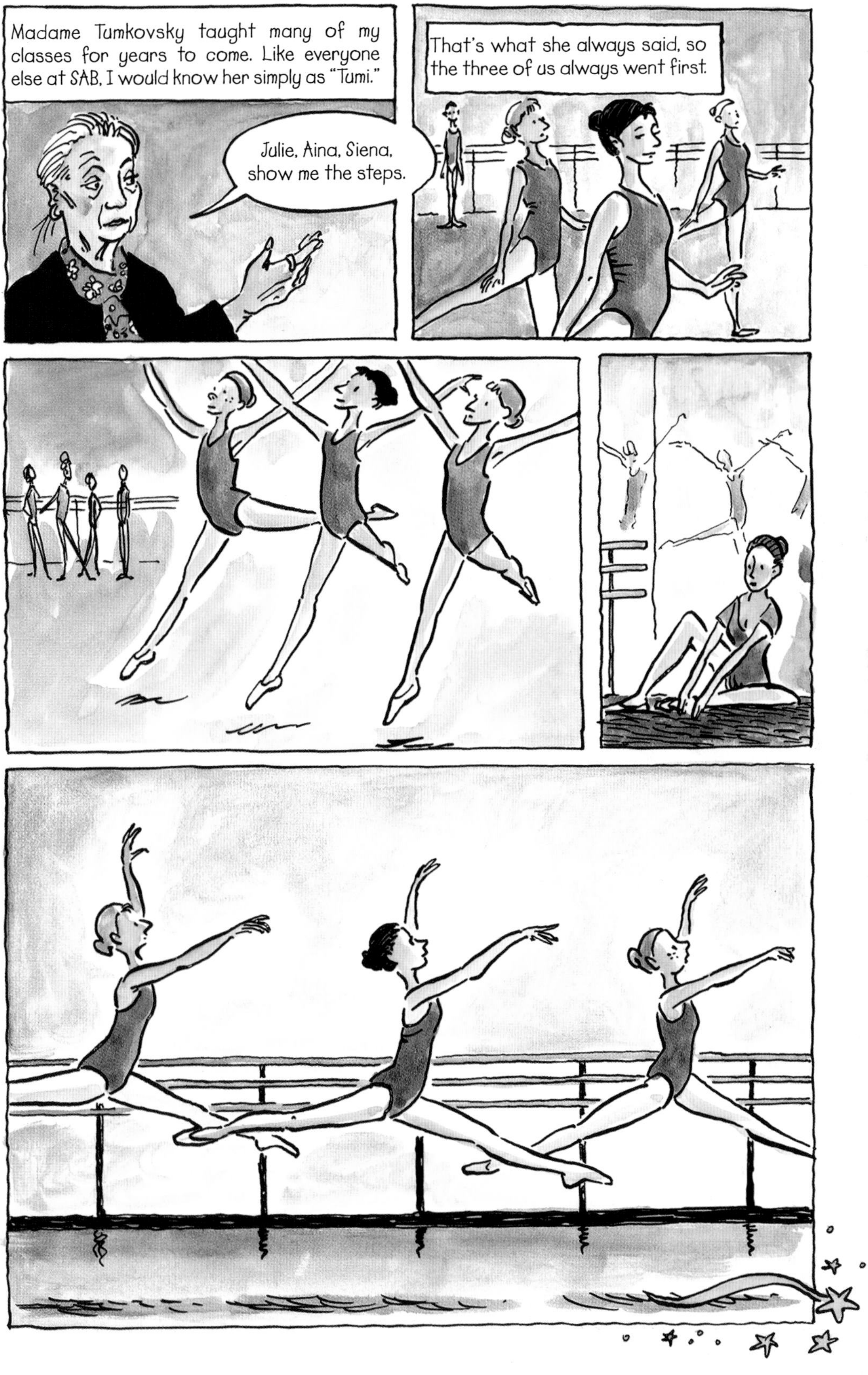
Madame Tumkovsky taught many of my classes for years to come. Like everyone else at SAB, I would know her simply as "Tumi."
Julie, Aina, Siena, show me the steps.
That's what she always said, so the three of us always went first.

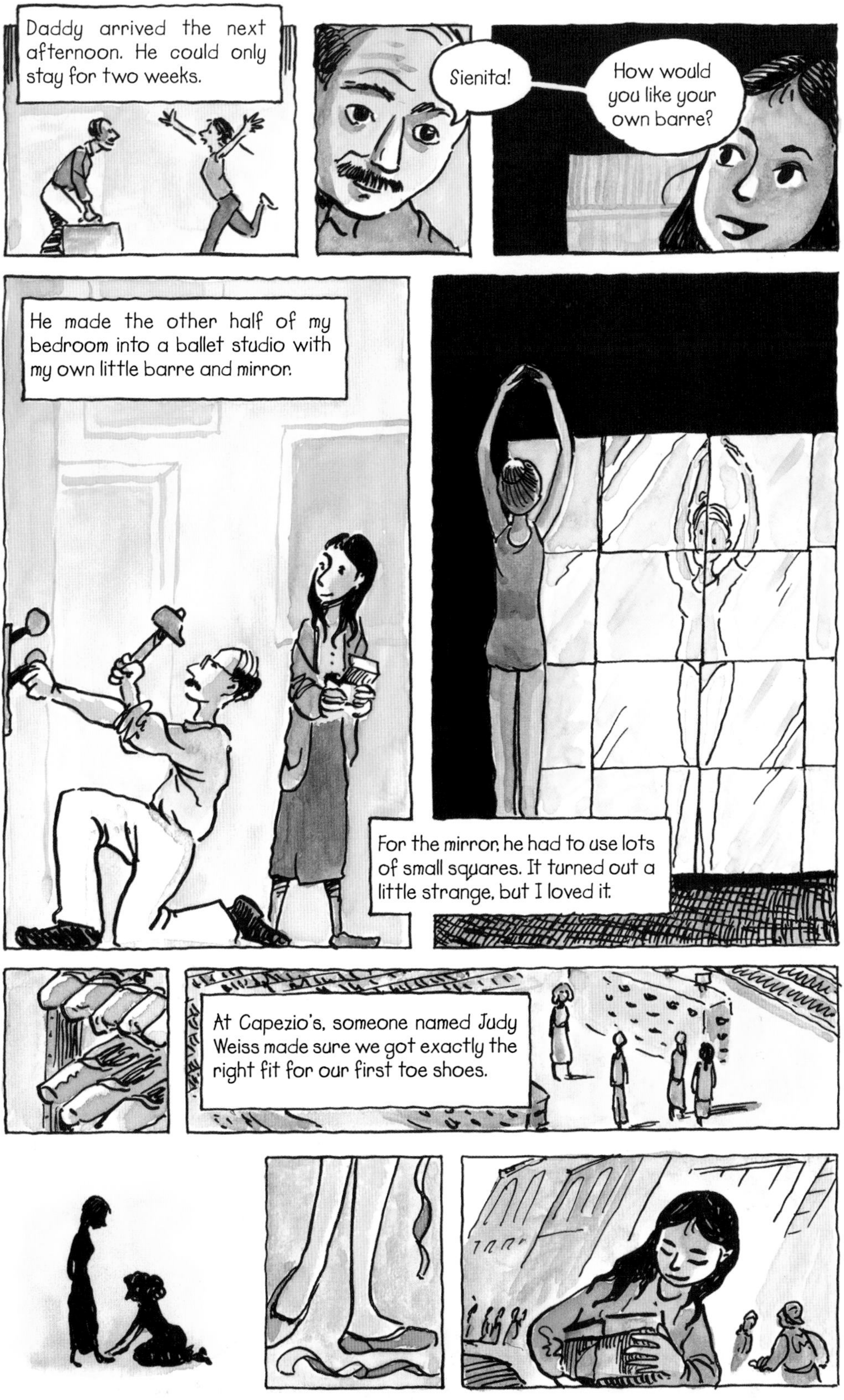
Daddy arrived the next afternoon. He could only stay for two weeks.
Sienita!
How would you like your own barre?
He made the other half of my bedroom into a ballet studio with my own little barre and mirror.
For the mirror, he had to use lots of small squares. It turned out a little strange, but I loved it.
At Capezio's, someone named Judy Weiss made sure we got exactly the right fit for our first toe shoes.

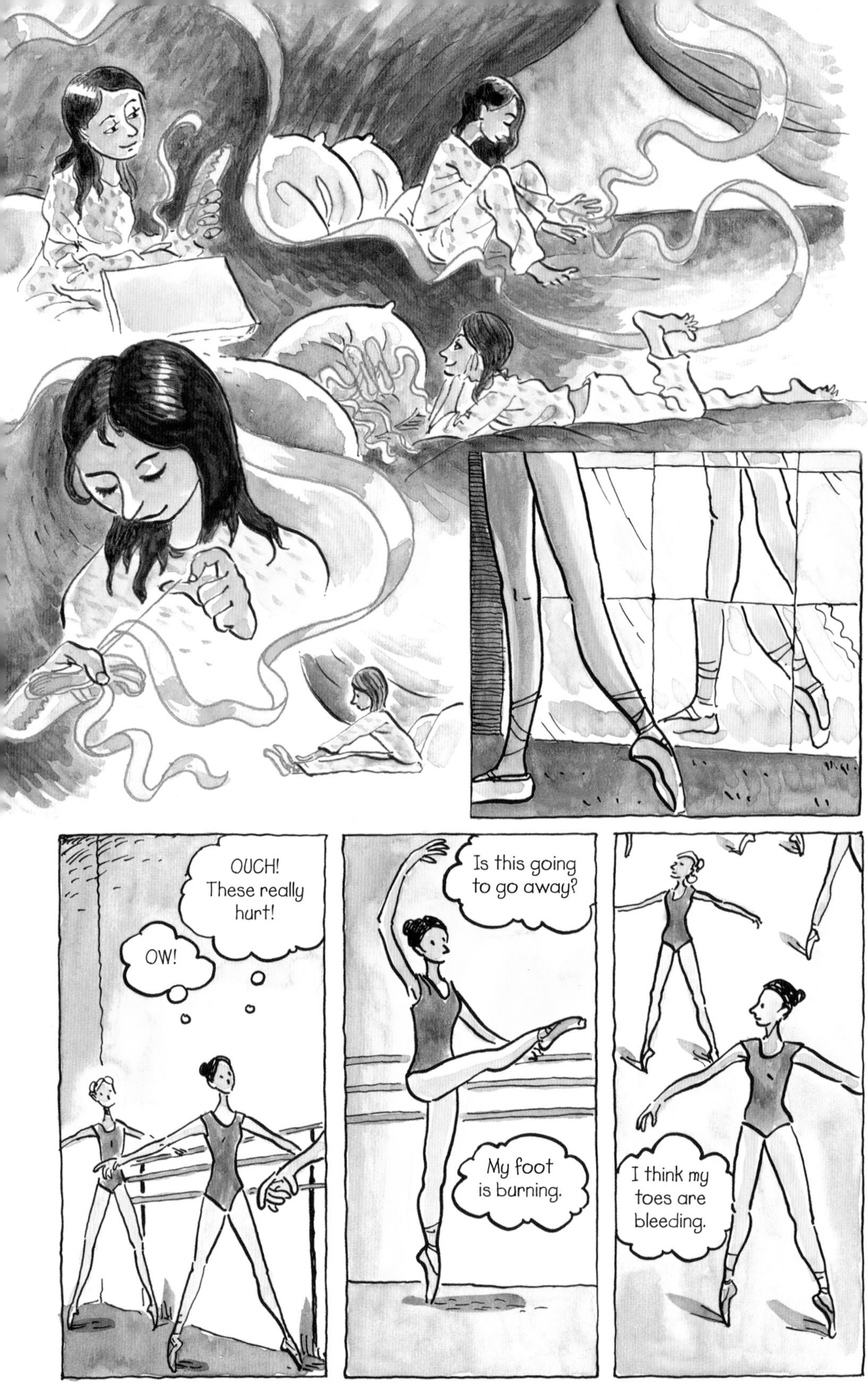
OUCH! These really hurt!
OW!
Is this going to go away?
My foot is burning.
I think my toes are bleeding.

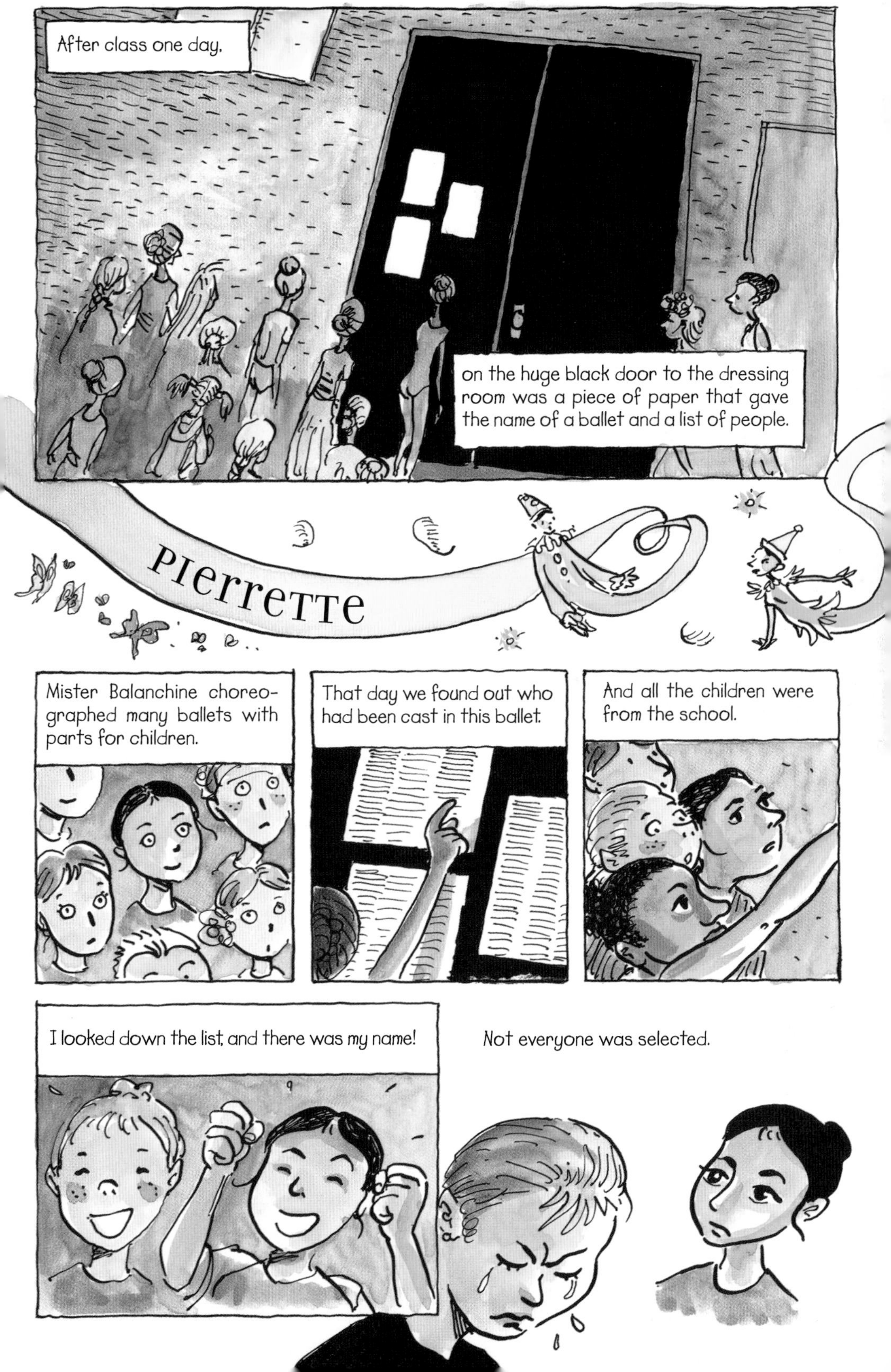
After class one day,
on the huge black door to the dressing room was a piece of paper that gave the name of a ballet and a list of people.
PIERRETTE
Mister Balanchine choreographed many ballets with parts for children.
That day we found out who had been cast in this ballet.
And all the children were from the school.
I looked down the list, and there was my name!
Not everyone was selected.

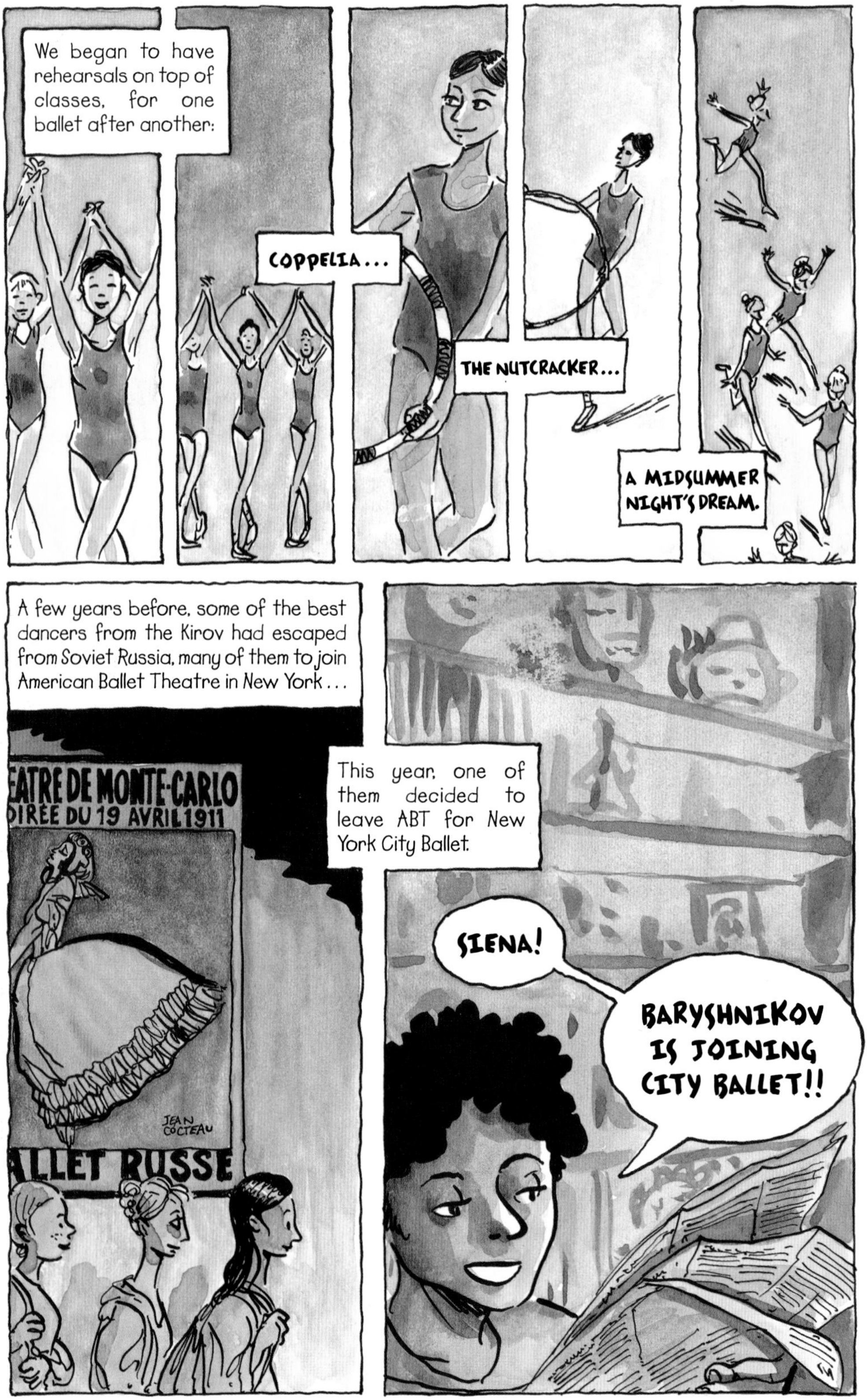
We began to have rehearsals on top of classes, for one ballet after another:
COPPELIA...
THE NUTCRACKER...
A MIDSUMMER NIGHT'S DREAM.
A few years before, some of the best dancers from the Kirov had escaped from Soviet Russia, many of them to join American Ballet Theatre in New York...
EATRE DE MONTE-CARLO
OIRÉE DU 19 AVRIL 1911
JEAN COCTEAU
ALLET RUSSE
This year, one of them decided to leave ABT for New York City Ballet.
SIENA!
BARYSHNIKOV IS JOINING CITY BALLET!!

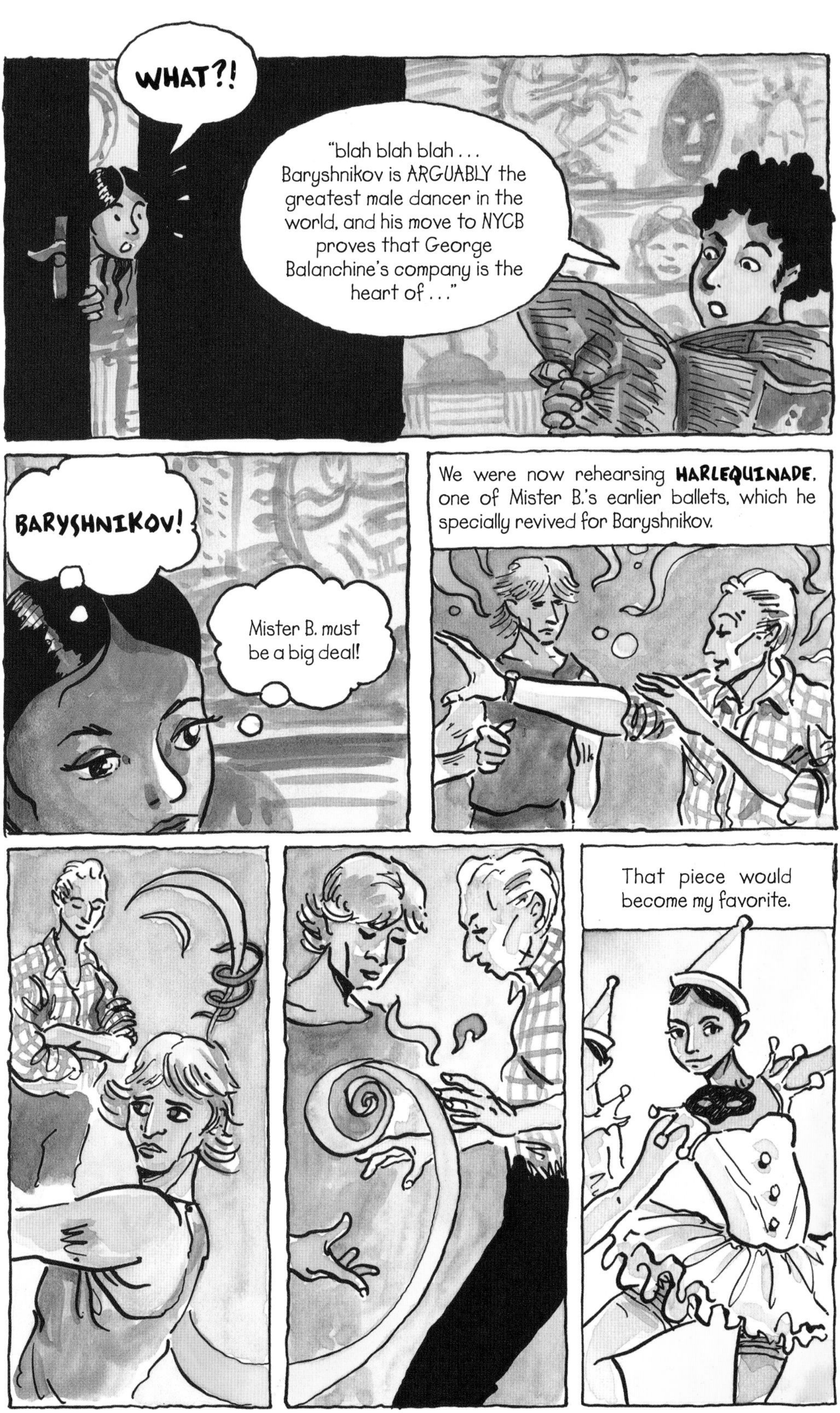
WHAT?!
"blah blah blah . . . Baryshnikov is ARGUABLY the greatest male dancer in the world, and his move to NYCB proves that George Balanchine's company is the heart of . . ."
BARYSHNIKOV!
Mister B. must be a big deal!
We were now rehearsing HARLEQUINADE, one of Mister B.'s earlier ballets, which he specially revived for Baryshnikov.
That piece would become my favorite.

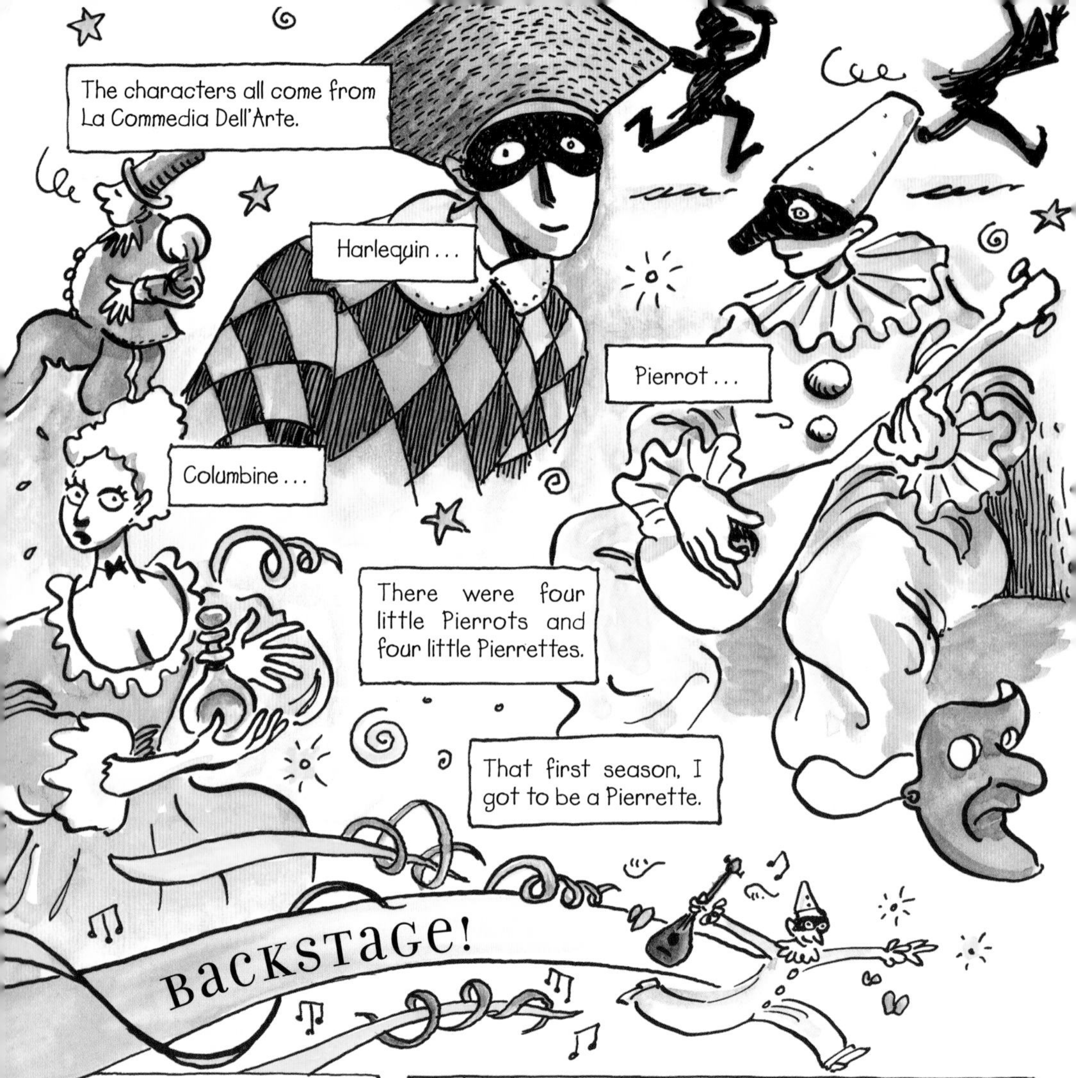
The characters all come from La Commedia Dell'Arte.
Harlequin . . .
Pierrot . . .
Columbine . . .
There were four little Pierrots and four little Pierrettes.
That first season, I got to be a Pierrette.
BACKSTAGE!

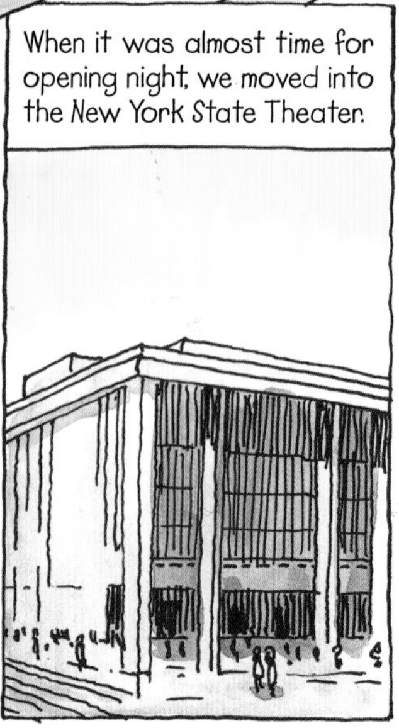
When it was almost time for opening night, we moved into the New York State Theater.

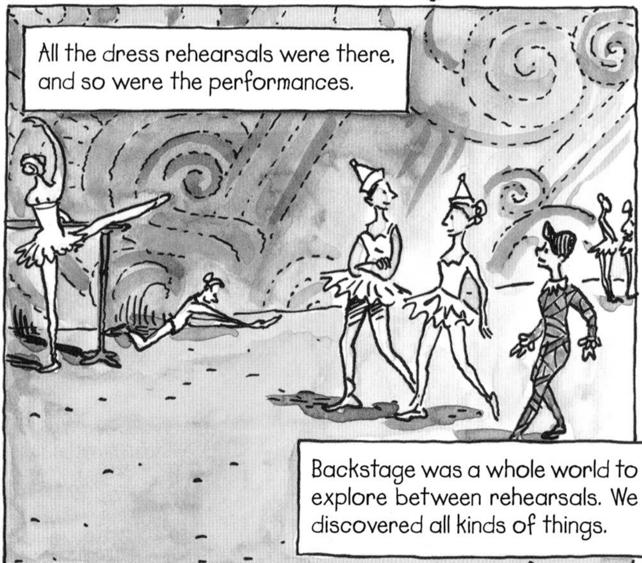
All the dress rehearsals were there, and so were the performances.
Backstage was a whole world to explore between rehearsals. We discovered all kinds of things.

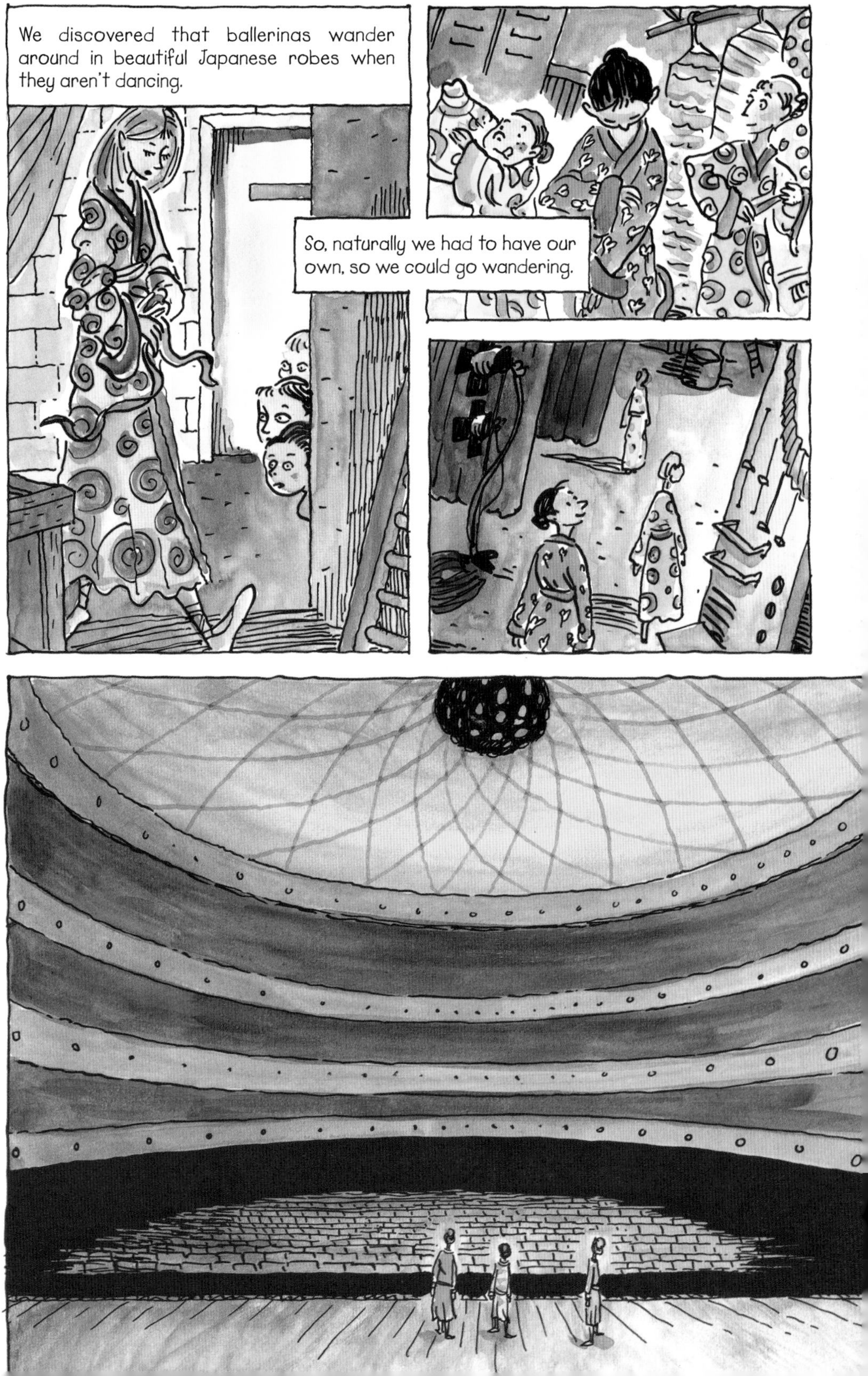
We discovered that ballerinas wander around in beautiful Japanese robes when they aren't dancing.
So, naturally we had to have our own, so we could go wandering.

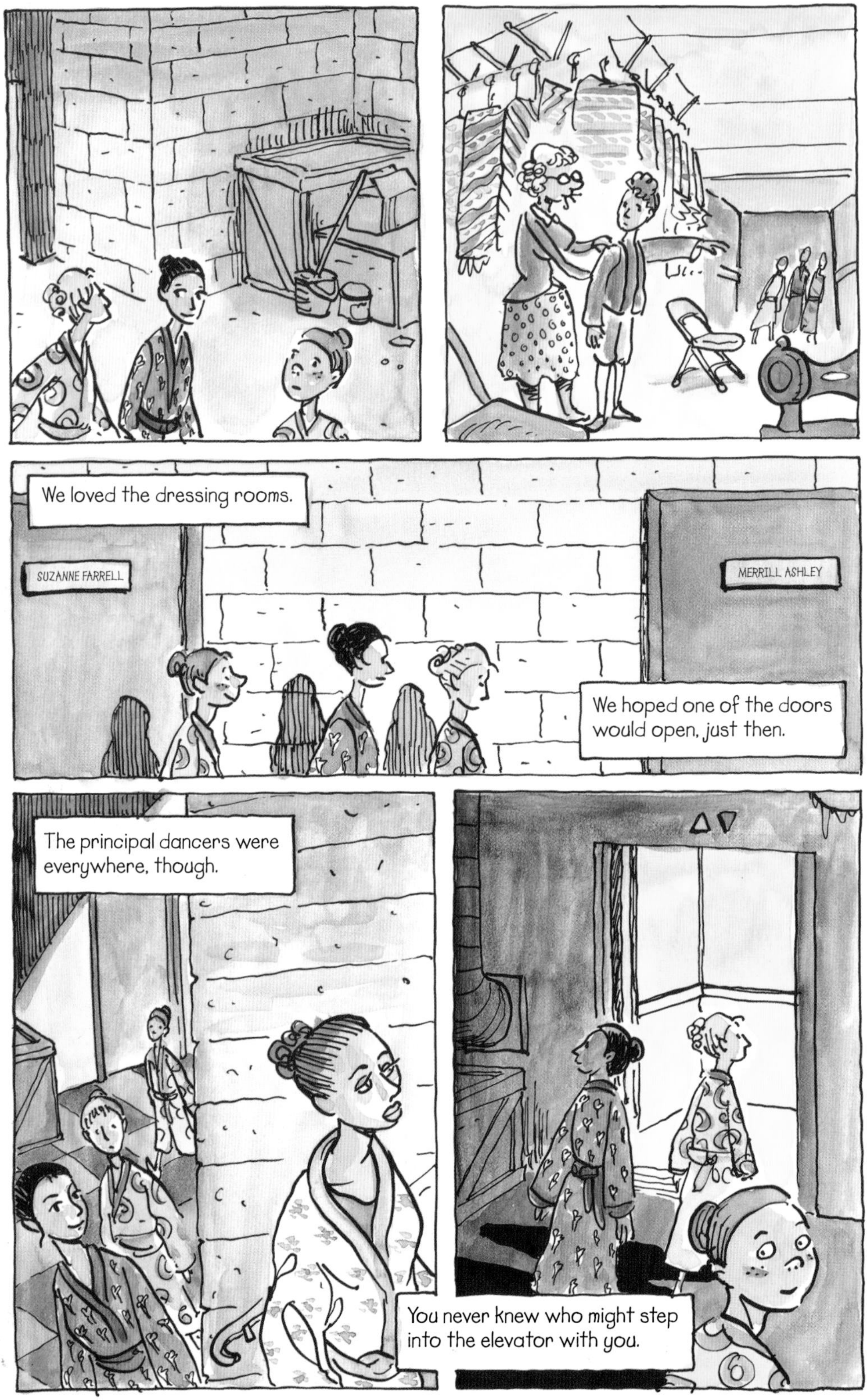
We loved the dressing rooms.
SUZANNE FARRELL
MERRILL ASHLEY
We hoped one of the doors would open, just then.
The principal dancers were everywhere, though.
You never knew who might step into the elevator with you.

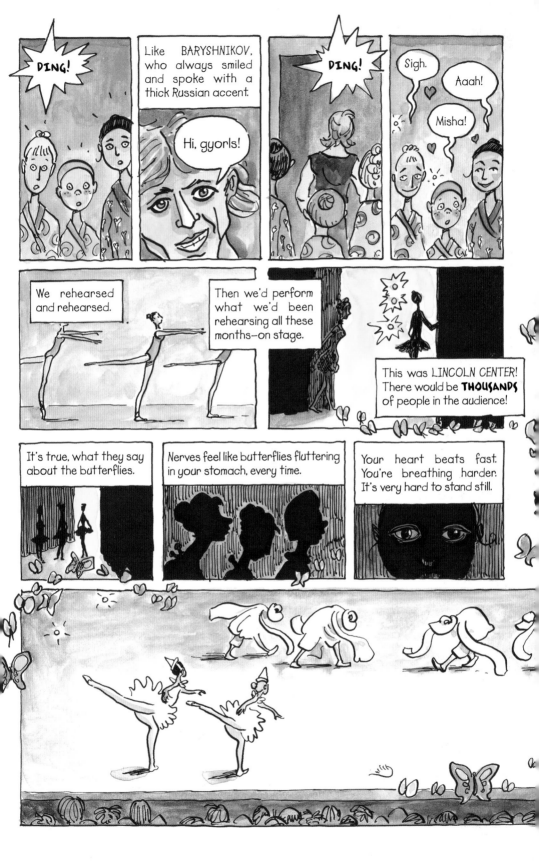

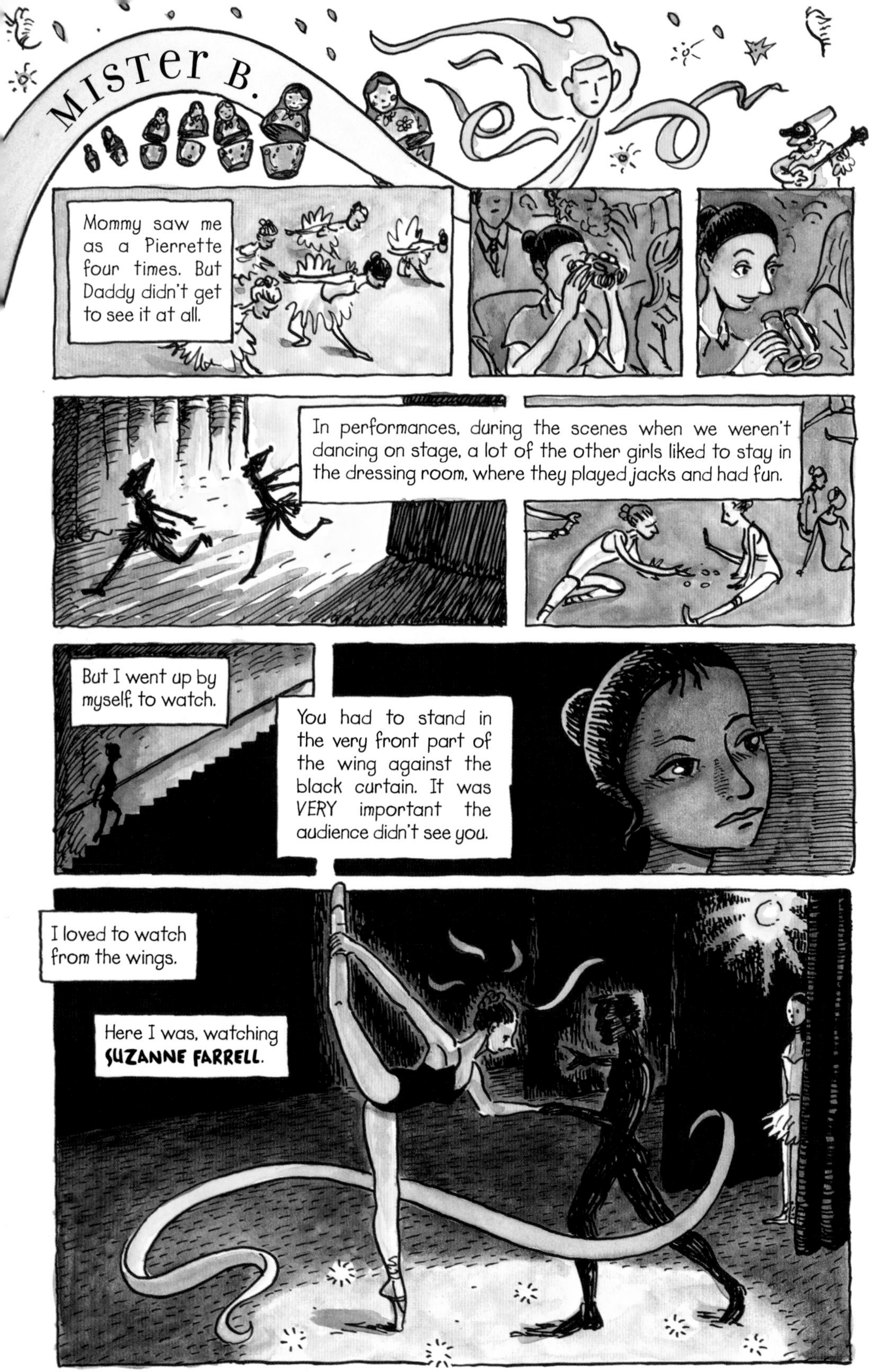
MISTER B.
Mommy saw me as a Pierrette four times. But Daddy didn't get to see it at all.
In performances, during the scenes when we weren't dancing on stage, a lot of the other girls liked to stay in the dressing room, where they played jacks and had fun.
But I went up by myself, to watch.
You had to stand in the very front part of the wing against the black curtain. It was VERY important the audience didn't see you.
I loved to watch from the wings.
Here I was, watching SUZANNE FARRELL.

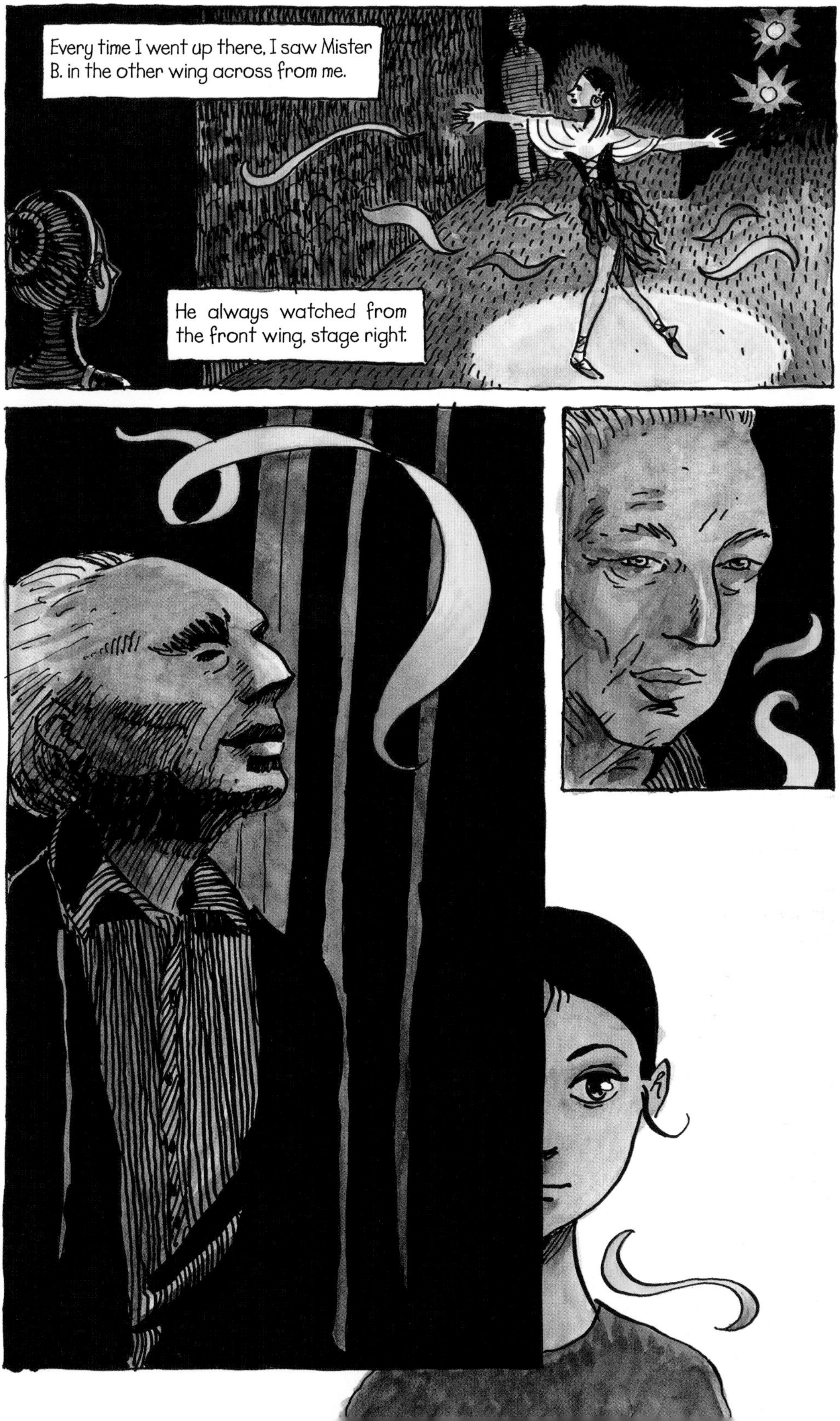
Every time I went up there, I saw Mister B. in the other wing across from me.
He always watched from the front wing, stage right.

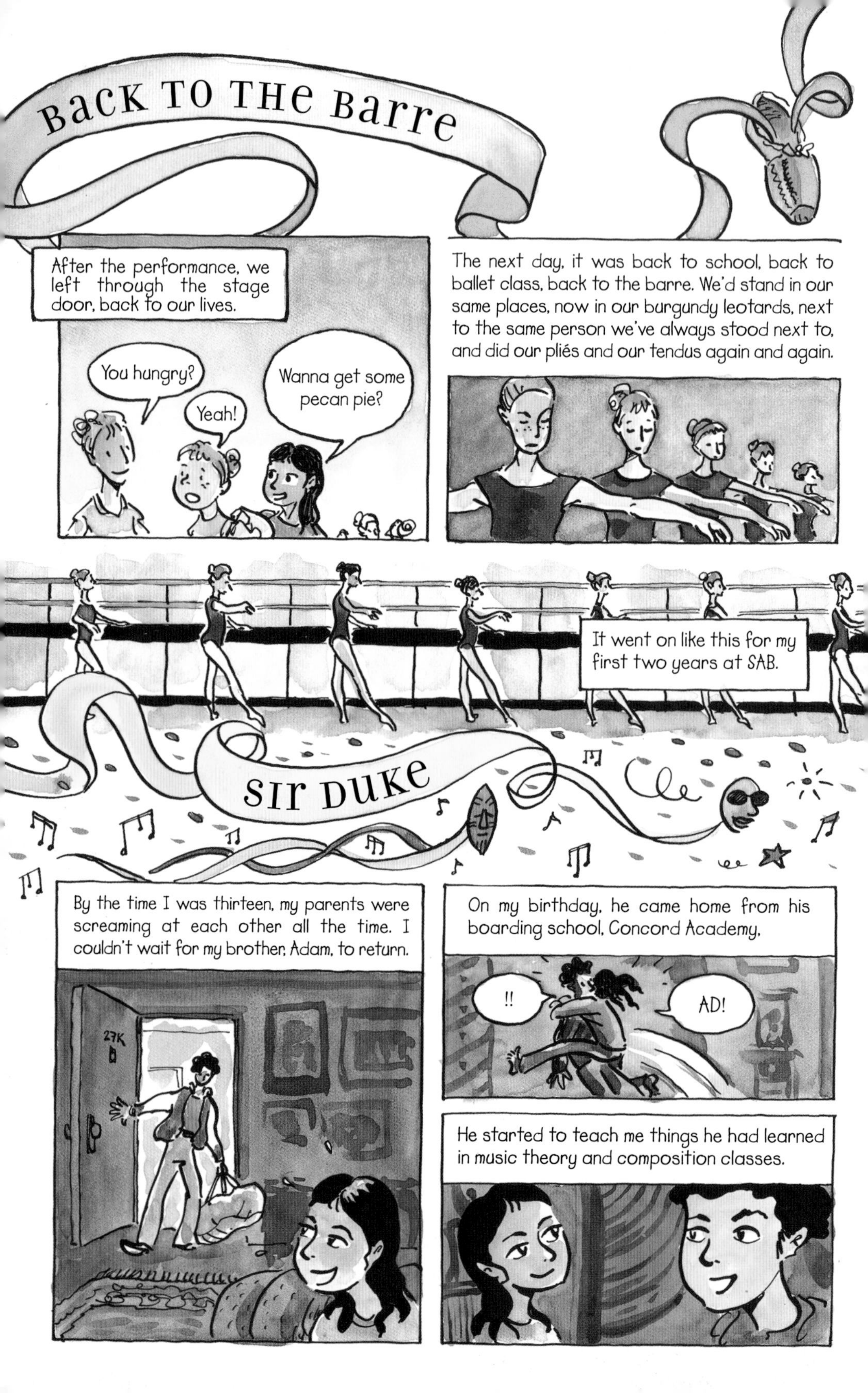
Back to the Barre
After the performance, we left through the stage door, back to our lives.
You hungry?
Yeah!
Wanna get some pecan pie?
The next day, it was back to school, back to ballet class, back to the barre. We'd stand in our same places, now in our burgundy leotards, next to the same person we've always stood next to, and did our pliés and our tendus again and again.
It went on like this for my first two years at SAB.
Sir Duke
By the time I was thirteen, my parents were screaming at each other all the time. I couldn't wait for my brother, Adam, to return.
27K
On my birthday, he came home from his boarding school, Concord Academy.
!!
AD!
He started to teach me things he had learned in music theory and composition classes.

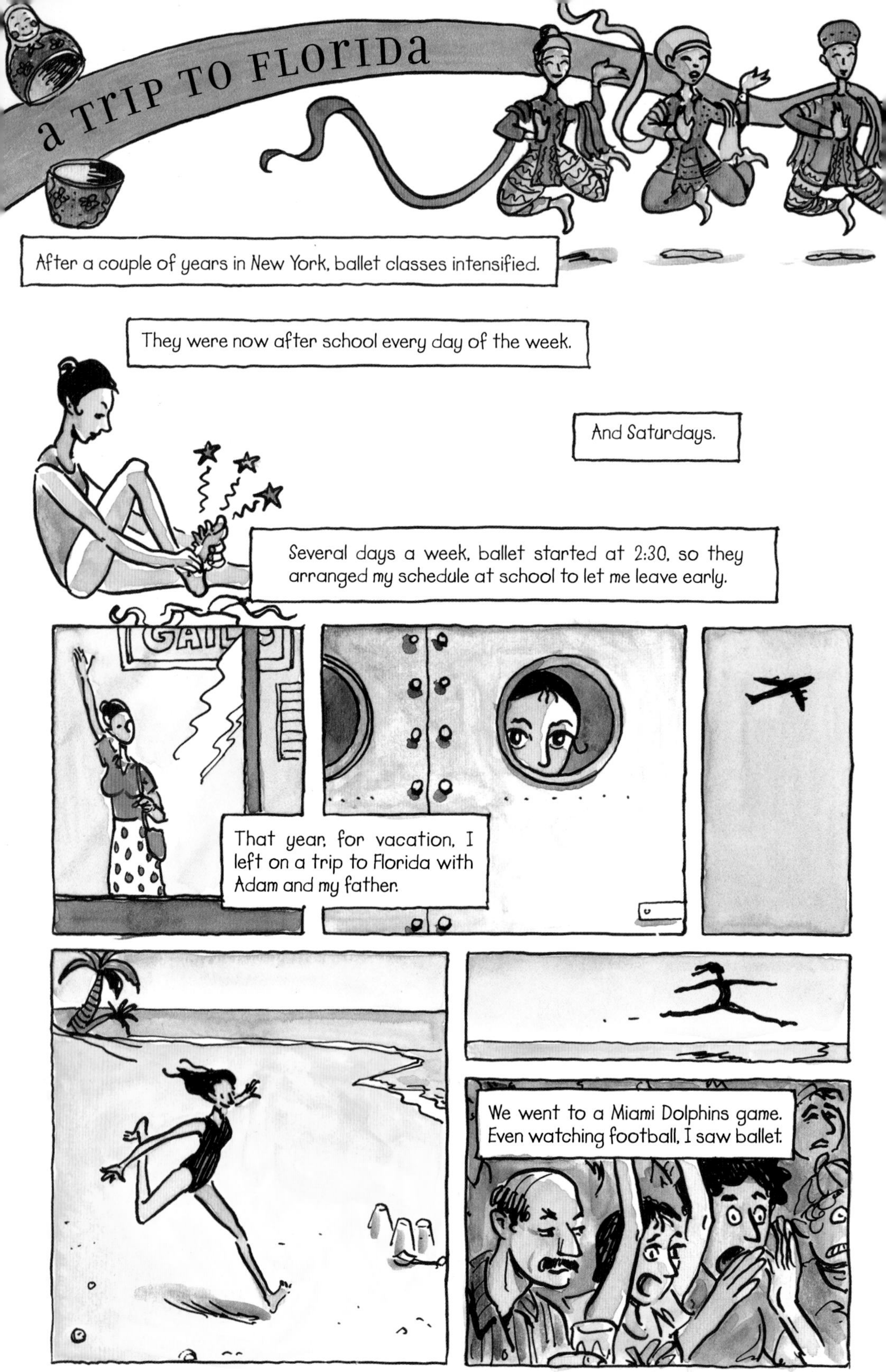
a Trip To FLorida
After a couple of years in New York, ballet classes intensified.
They were now after school every day of the week.
And Saturdays.
Several days a week, ballet started at 2:30, so they arranged my schedule at school to let me leave early.
GATE
That year, for vacation, I left on a trip to Florida with Adam and my father.
We went to a Miami Dolphins game. Even watching football, I saw ballet.

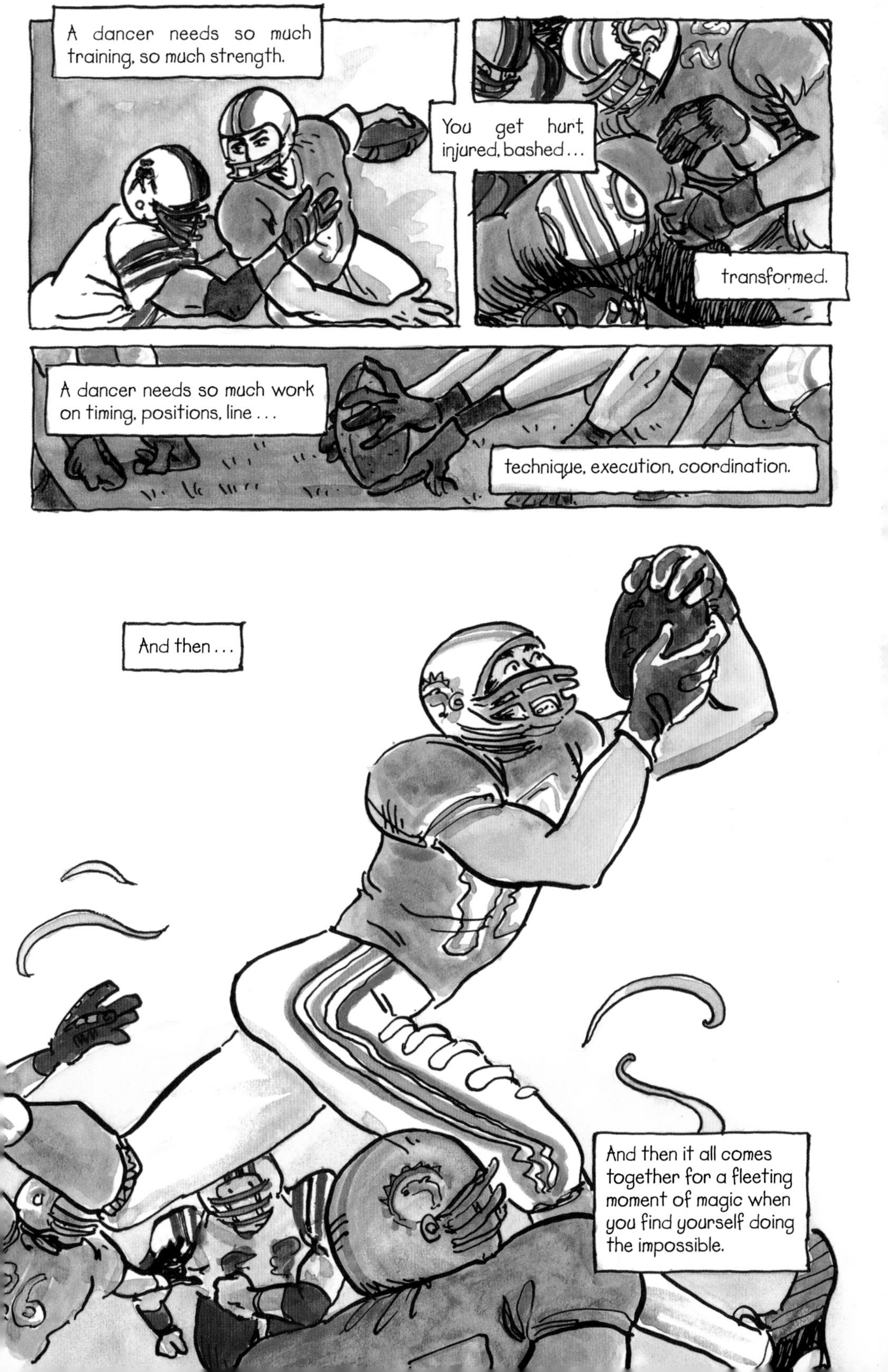
A dancer needs so much training, so much strength.
You get hurt, injured, bashed . . .
transformed.
A dancer needs so much work on timing, positions, line . . .
technique, execution, coordination.
And then . . .
And then it all comes together for a fleeting moment of magic when you find yourself doing the impossible.

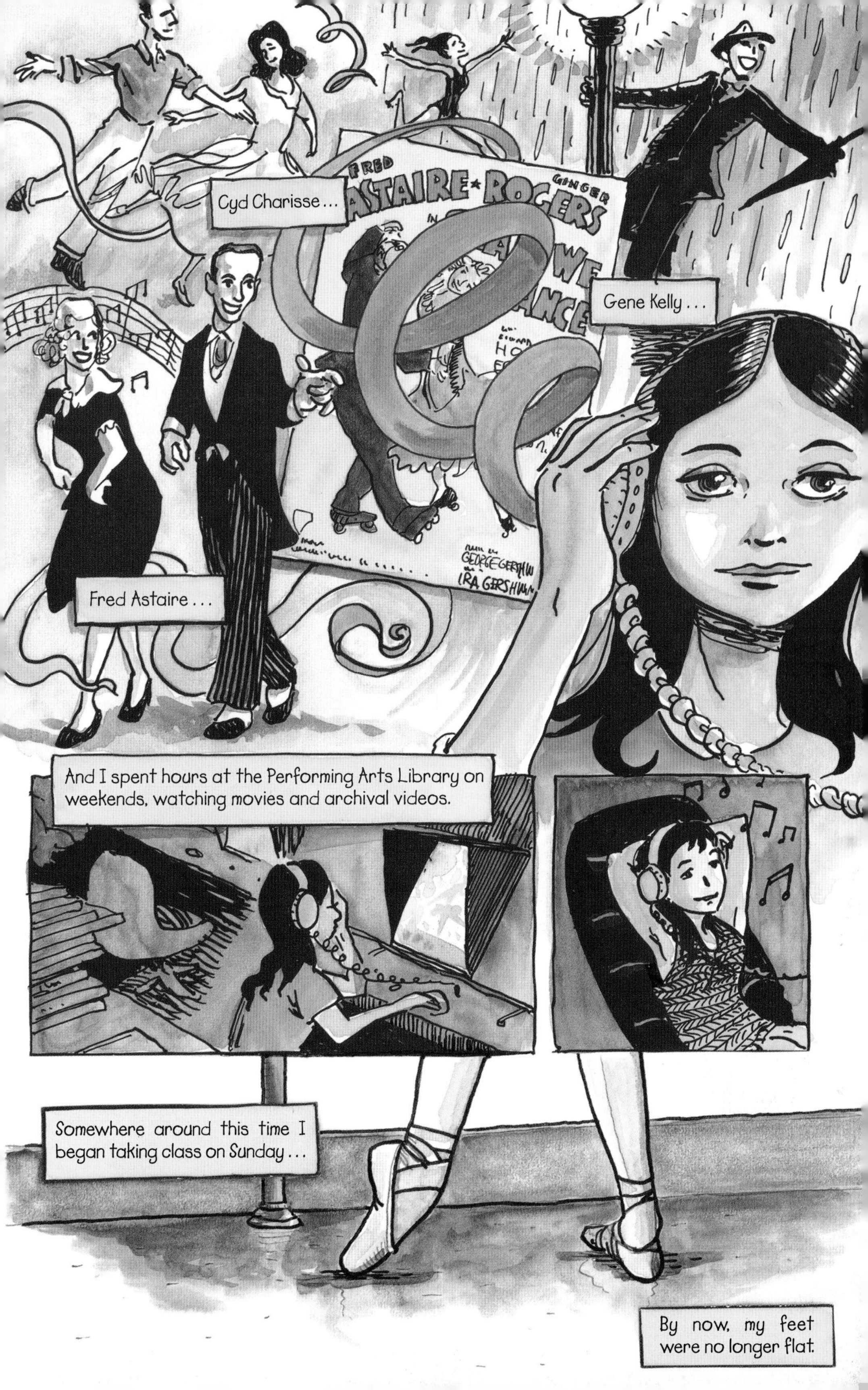
FRED
GINGER
ASTAIRE ★ ROGERS
Cyd Charisse . . .
Gene Kelly . . .
Fred Astaire . . .
GEORGE GERSHWIN
IRA GERSHWIN
And I spent hours at the Performing Arts Library on weekends, watching movies and archival videos.
Somewhere around this time I began taking class on Sunday . . .
By now, my feet were no longer flat.

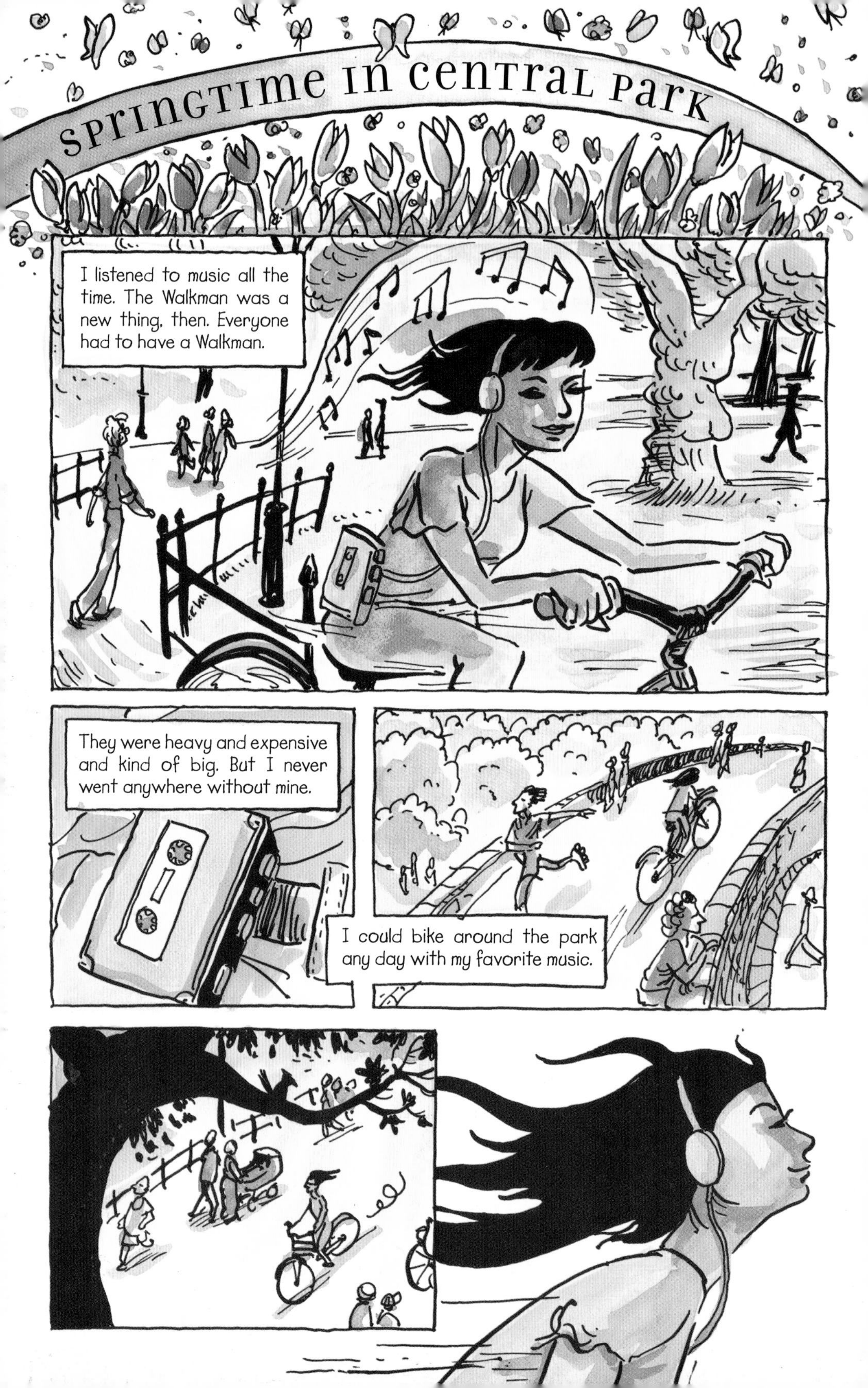
Springtime in Central Park
I listened to music all the time. The Walkman was a new thing, then. Everyone had to have a Walkman.
They were heavy and expensive and kind of big. But I never went anywhere without mine.
I could bike around the park any day with my favorite music.

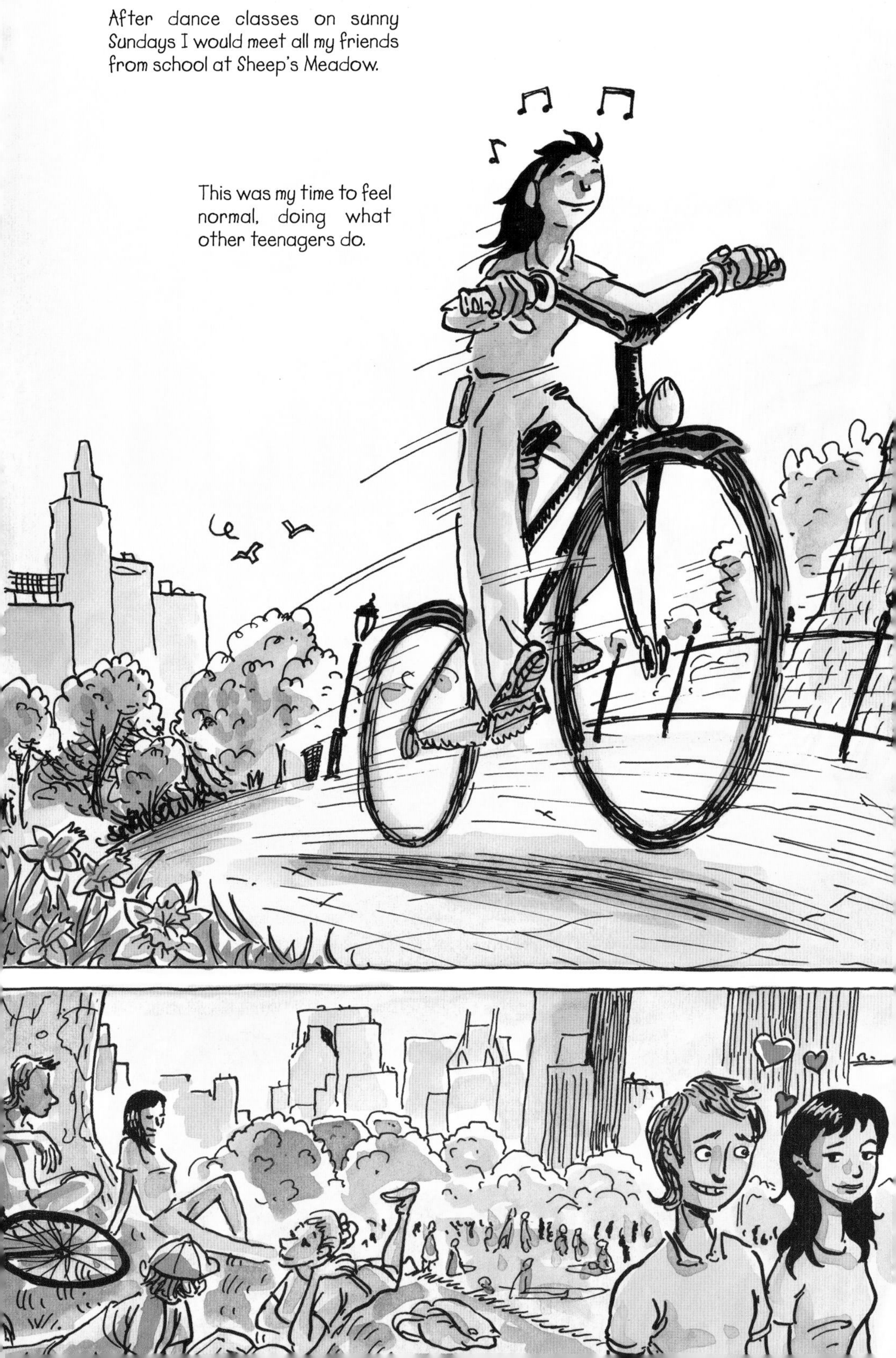
After dance classes on sunny Sundays I would meet all my friends from school at Sheep's Meadow.
This was my time to feel normal, doing what other teenagers do.

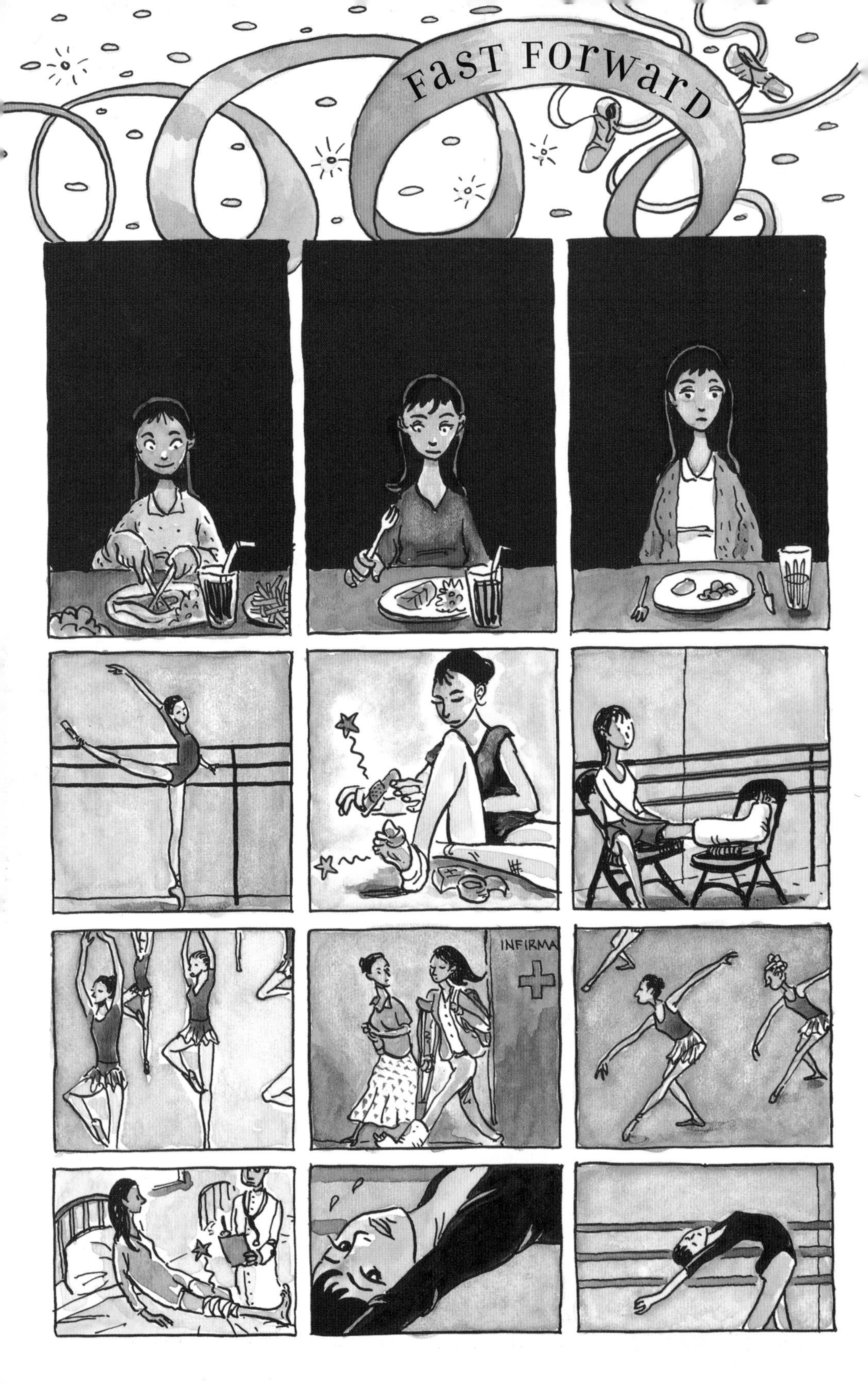
Fast Forward
INFIRMA

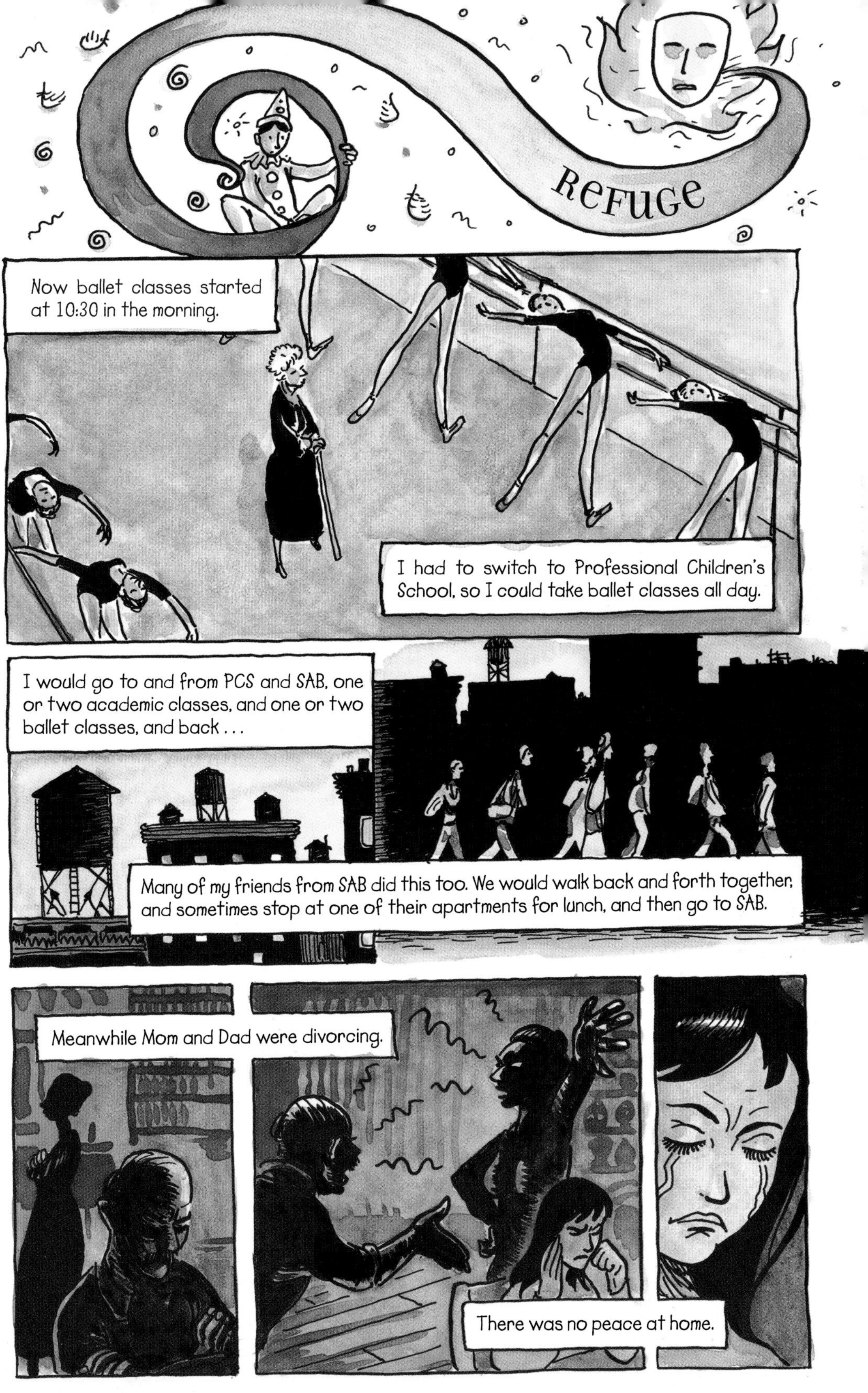
REFUGE
Now ballet classes started at 10:30 in the morning.
I had to switch to Professional Children's School, so I could take ballet classes all day.
I would go to and from PCS and SAB, one or two academic classes, and one or two ballet classes, and back . . .
Many of my friends from SAB did this too. We would walk back and forth together, and sometimes stop at one of their apartments for lunch, and then go to SAB.
Meanwhile Mom and Dad were divorcing.
There was no peace at home.

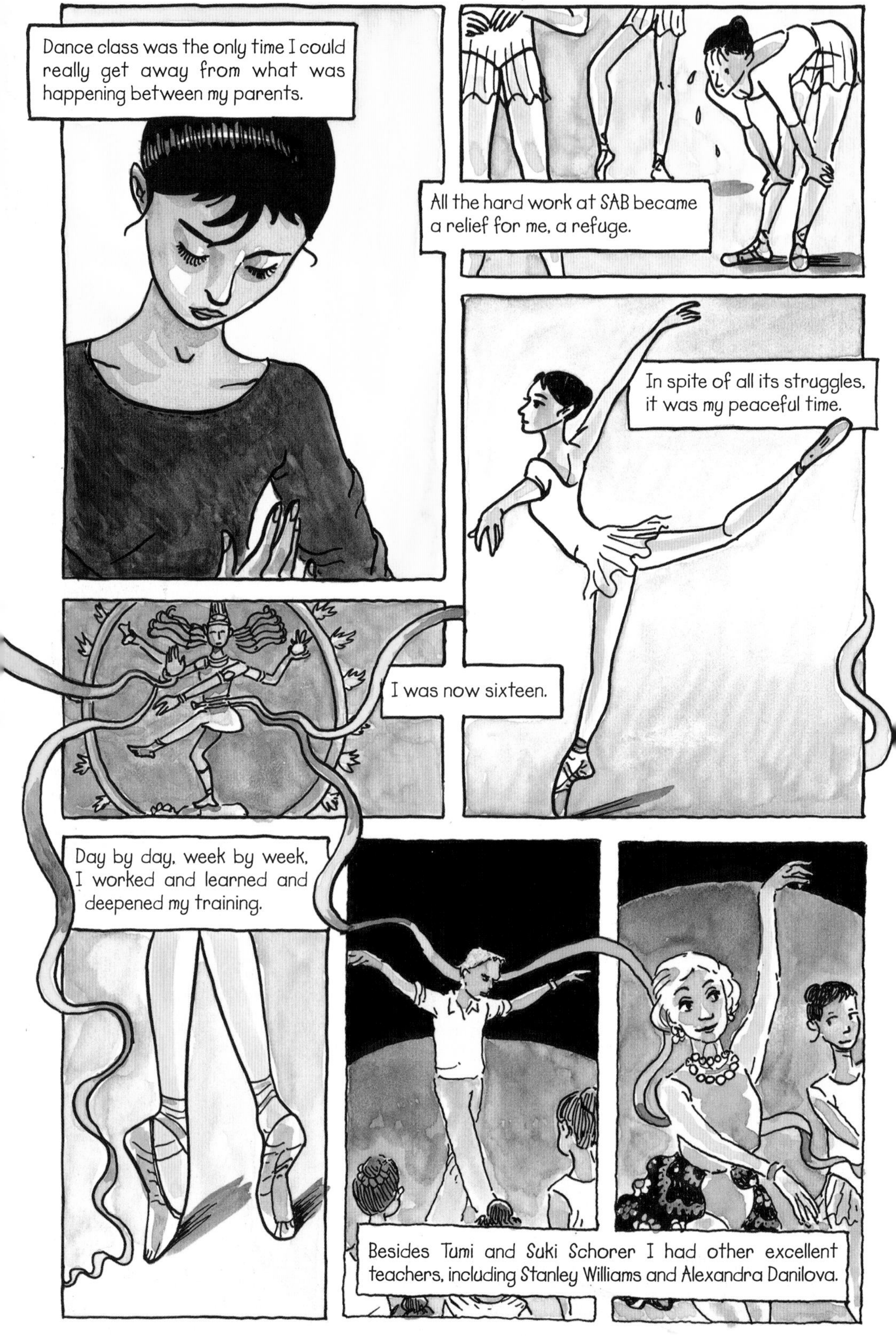
Dance class was the only time I could really get away from what was happening between my parents.
All the hard work at SAB became a relief for me, a refuge.
In spite of all its struggles, it was my peaceful time.
I was now sixteen.
Day by day, week by week, I worked and learned and deepened my training.
Besides Tumi and Suki Schorer I had other excellent teachers, including Stanley Williams and Alexandra Danilova.

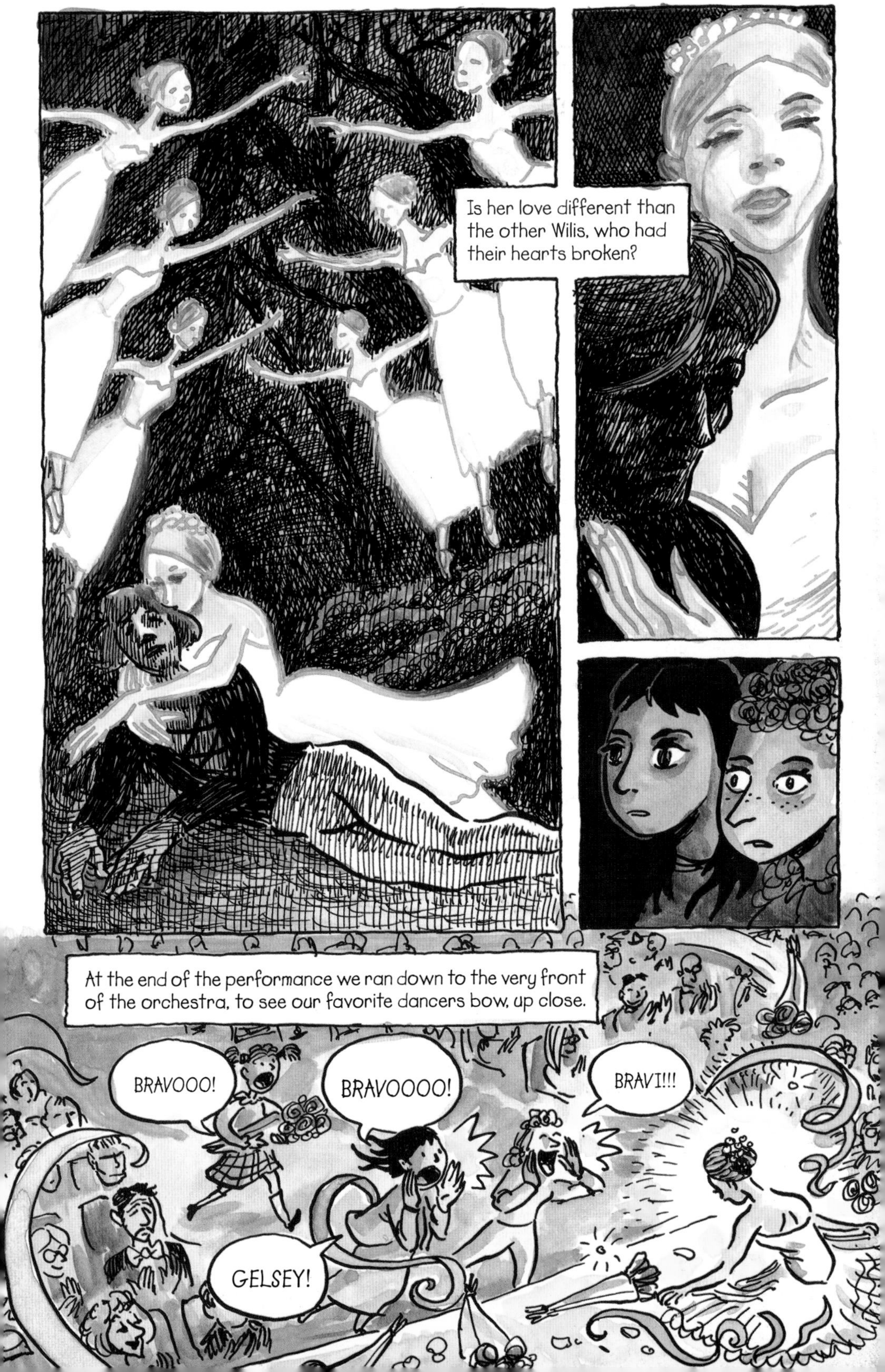
Is her love different than the other Wilis, who had their hearts broken?
At the end of the performance we ran down to the very front of the orchestra, to see our favorite dancers bow, up close.
BRAVOOO!
BRAVOOOO!
BRAVI!!!
GELSEY!

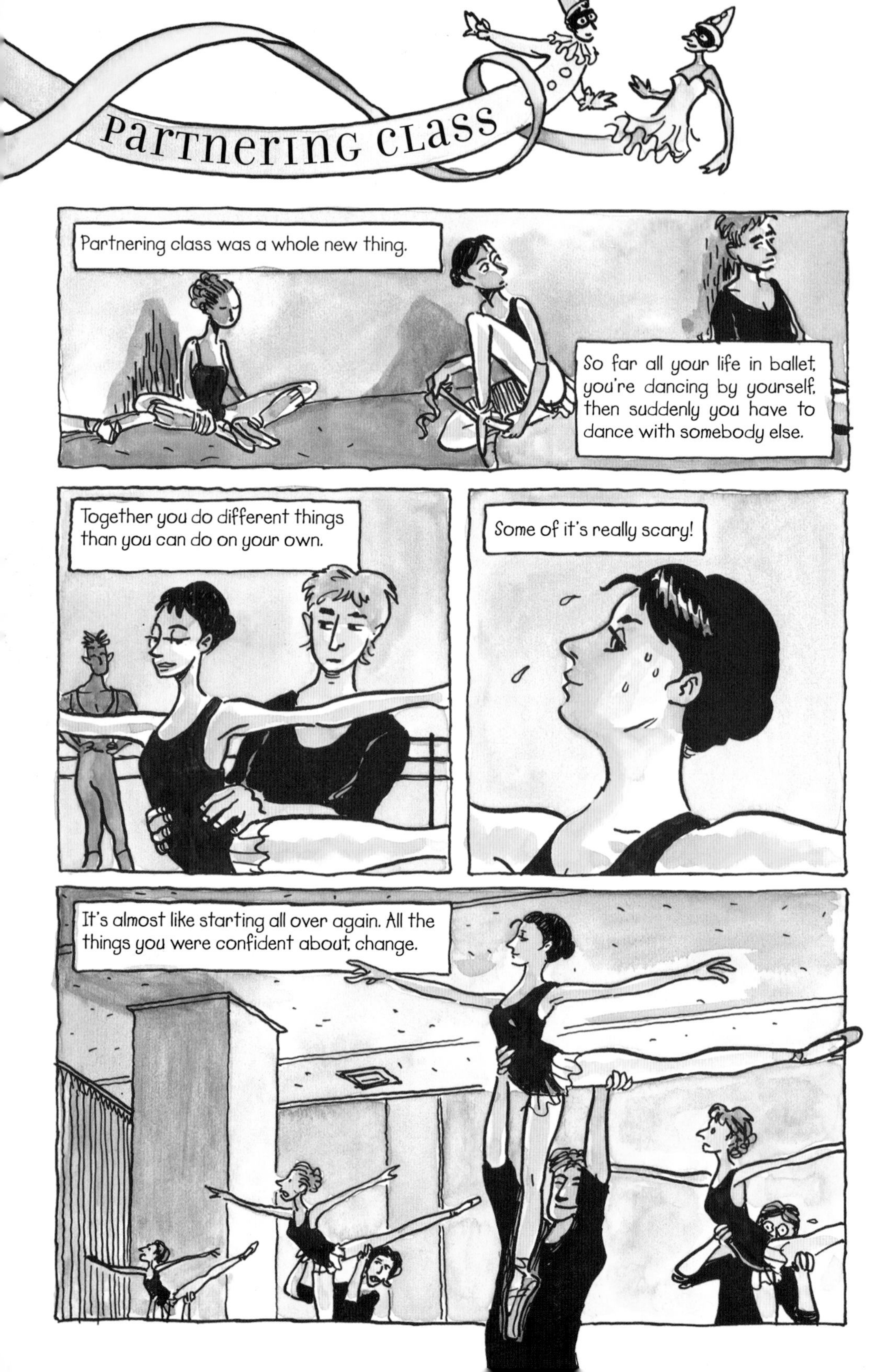
Partnering Class
Partnering class was a whole new thing.
So far all your life in ballet, you're dancing by yourself, then suddenly you have to dance with somebody else.
Together you do different things than you can do on your own.
Some of it's really scary!
It's almost like starting all over again. All the things you were confident about, change.

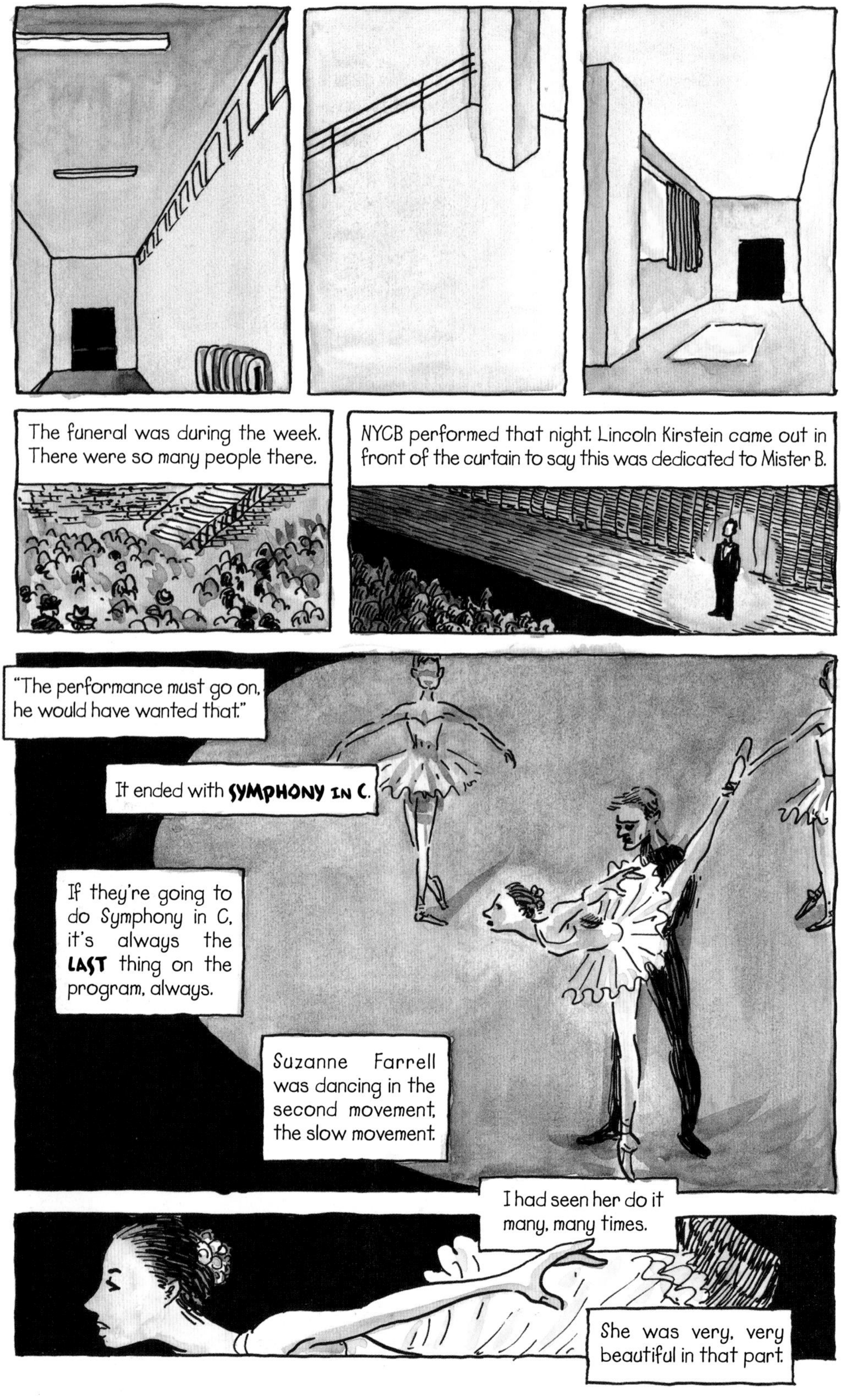
The funeral was during the week. There were so many people there.
NYCB performed that night. Lincoln Kirstein came out in front of the curtain to say this was dedicated to Mister B.
"The performance must go on, he would have wanted that."
It ended with SYMPHONY IN C.
If they're going to do Symphony in C, it's always the LAST thing on the program, always.
Suzanne Farrell was dancing in the second movement, the slow movement.
I had seen her do it many, many times.
She was very, very beautiful in that part.

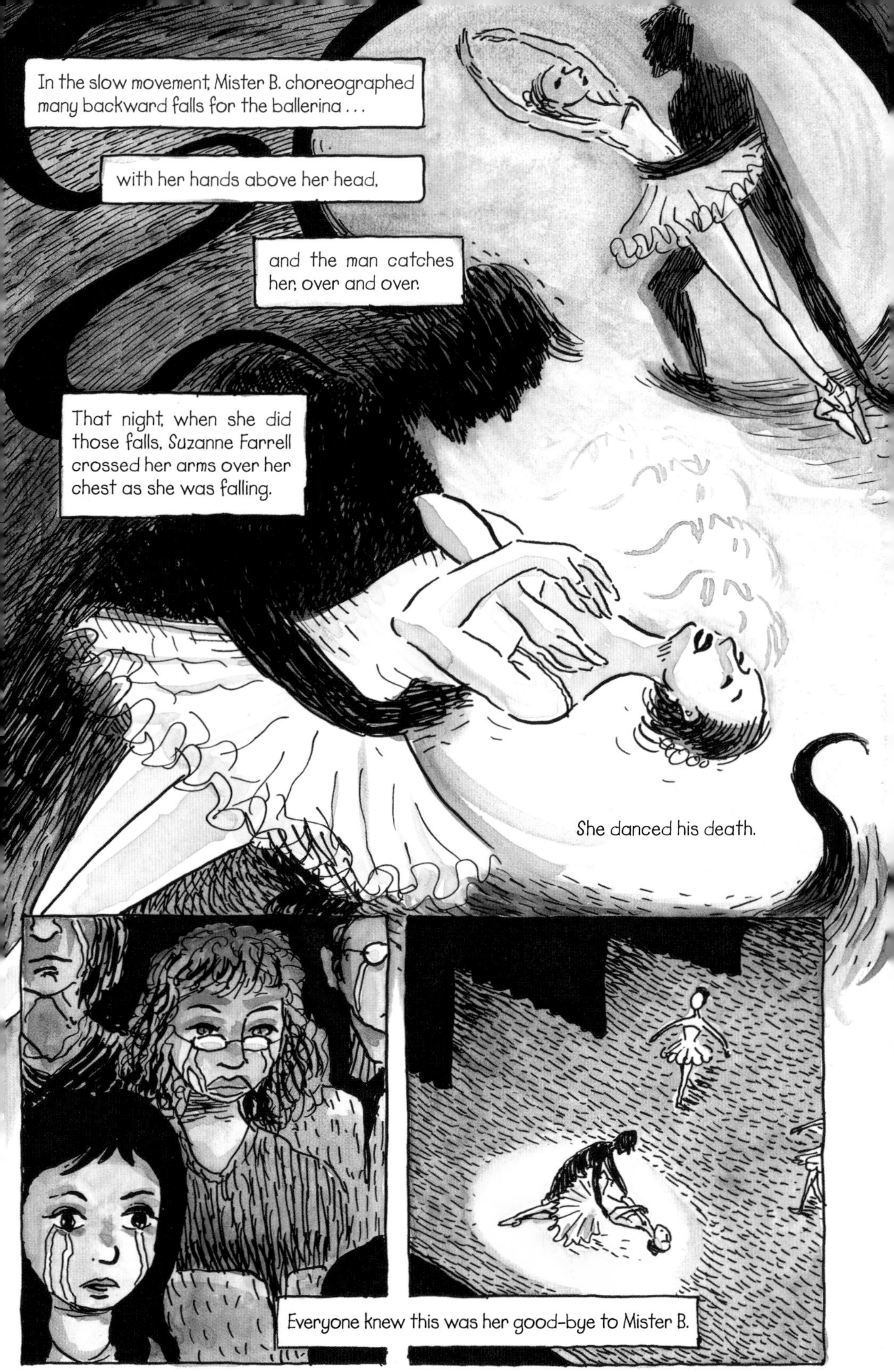
In the slow movement, Mister B. choreographed many backward falls for the ballerina . . .
with her hands above her head,
and the man catches her, over and over.
That night, when she did those falls, Suzanne Farrell crossed her arms over her chest as she was falling.
She danced his death.
Everyone knew this was her good-bye to Mister B.

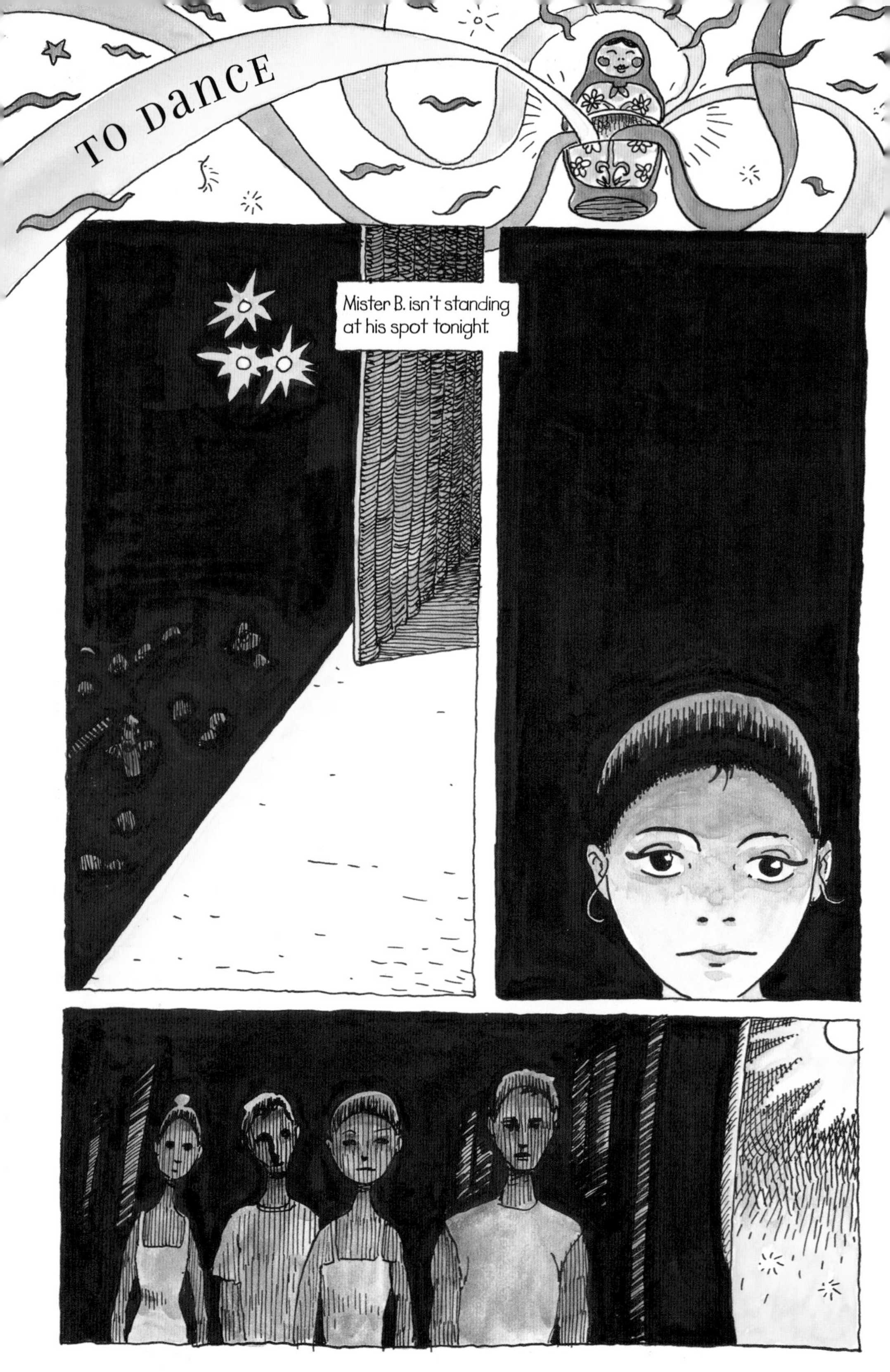
TO DANCE
Mister B. isn't standing at his spot tonight.

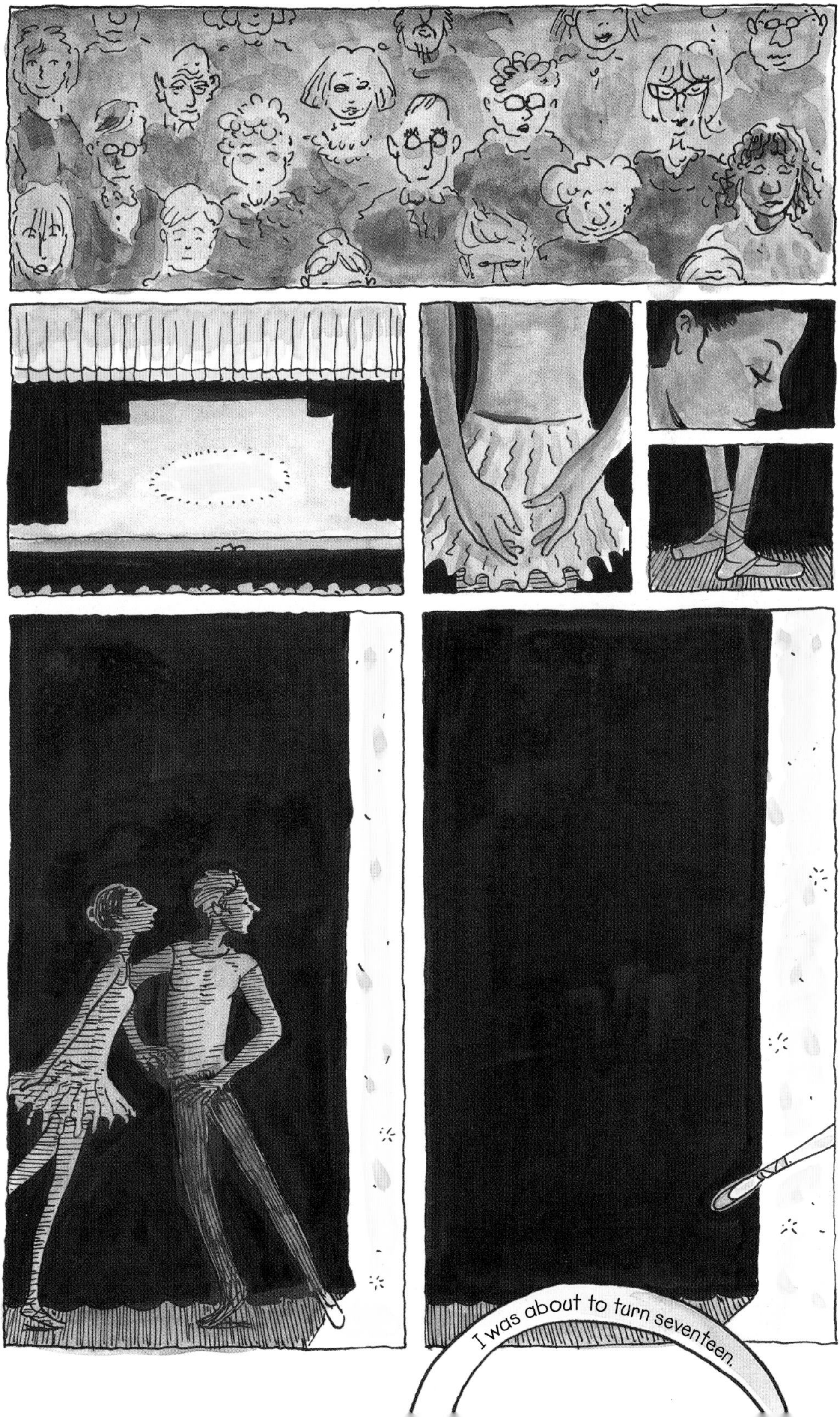
I was about to turn seventeen.

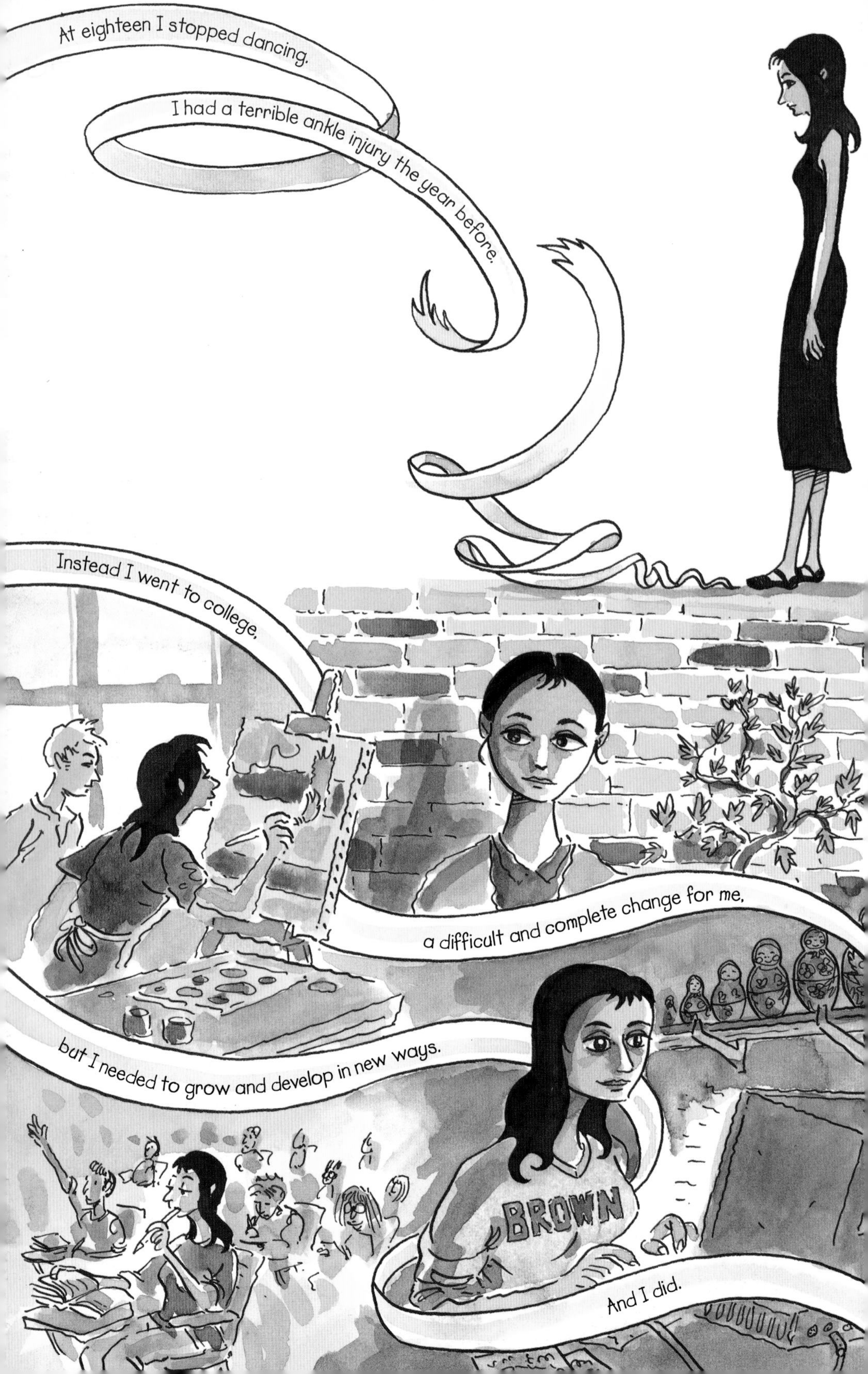

At eighteen I stopped dancing.
I had a terrible ankle injury the year before.
Instead I went to college,
a difficult and complete change for me,
but I needed to grow and develop in new ways.
And I did.
BROWN

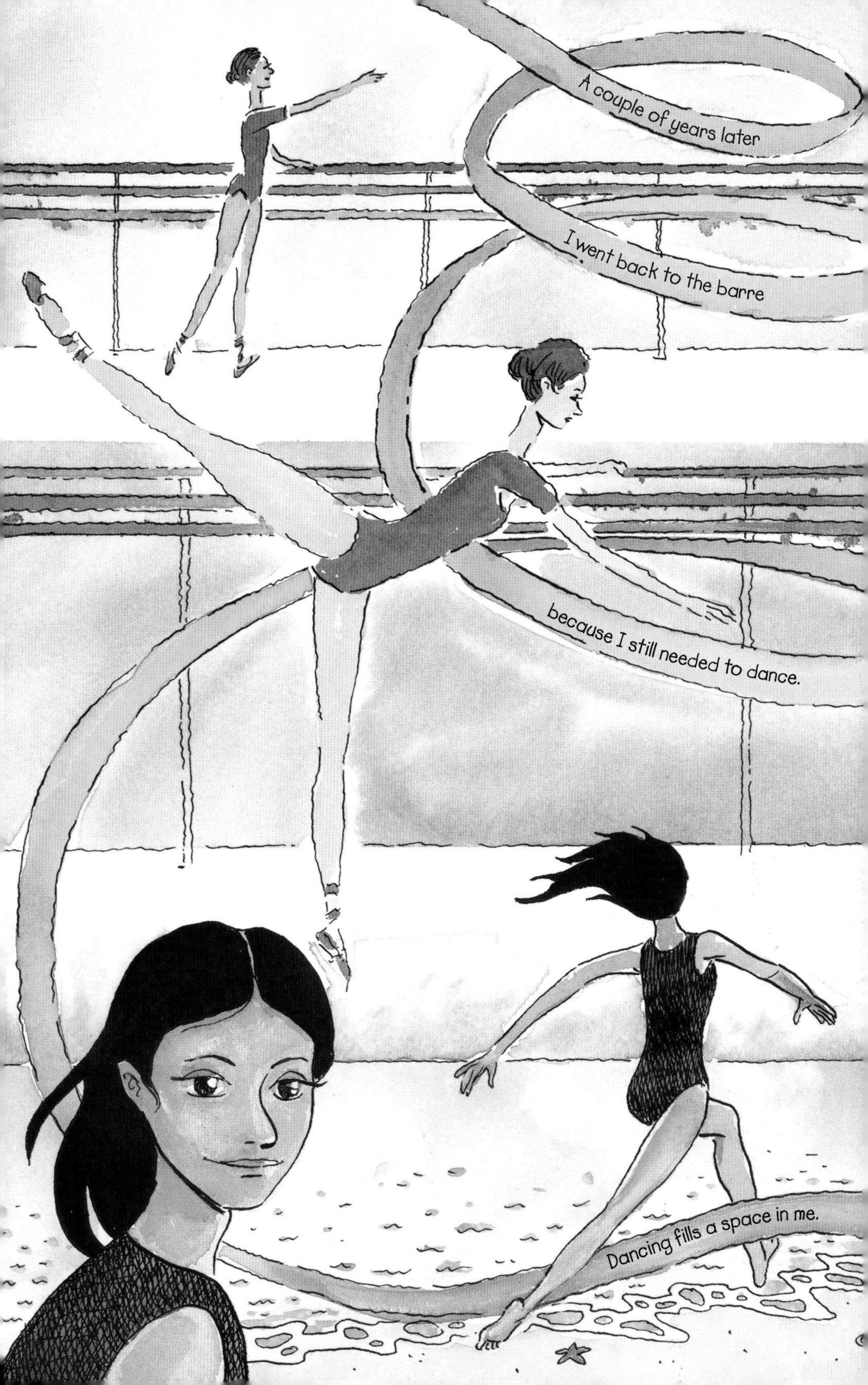
A couple of years later
I went back to the barre
because I still needed to dance.
Dancing fills a space in me.

ACKNOWLEDGMENTS

Special thanks to Adam Cherson and Lee Wade, and

Many, many thanks to Ann Bobco, Tanya McKinnon, Rebecca Wright, Yuri Kucherov, Kristy Raffensberger, Sonia Chaghatzbanian, Michael McCartney, Jeannie Ng, Emma Dryden, and Alexis Siegel.

ALADDIN PAPERBACKS
An imprint of Simon & Schuster
Children's Publishing Division
1230 Avenue of the Americas
New York, New York 10020
Text copyright © 2006 by Siena Siegel
Illustrations copyright © 2006 by Mark Siegel
A Very Young Dancer by Jill Krementz is reproduced
on pp. 15 and 26 with permission from the author,
who controls all rights.
Symphony in C, choreography by George Balanchine
© School of American Ballet.
*Agon, A Midsummer Night's Dream, Coppelia,
Harlequinade, George Balanchine's The Nutcracker™,*
and *Tzigane*, choreography by George Balanchine
© The George Balanchine Trust.
Balanchine is a registered trademark of The George
Balanchine Trust.
Also available in Atheneum Books for
Young Readers hardcover edition.
Book design by Mark Siegel
The text for this book is set in Lemonade
and Housepaint.
The illustrations for this book are rendered in
watercolor and ink.
Manufactured in China
10
CIP data for this book is available
from the Library of Congress.
ISBN-13: 978-1-4169-2687-0
ISBN-10: 1-4169-2687-9
1014 SCP

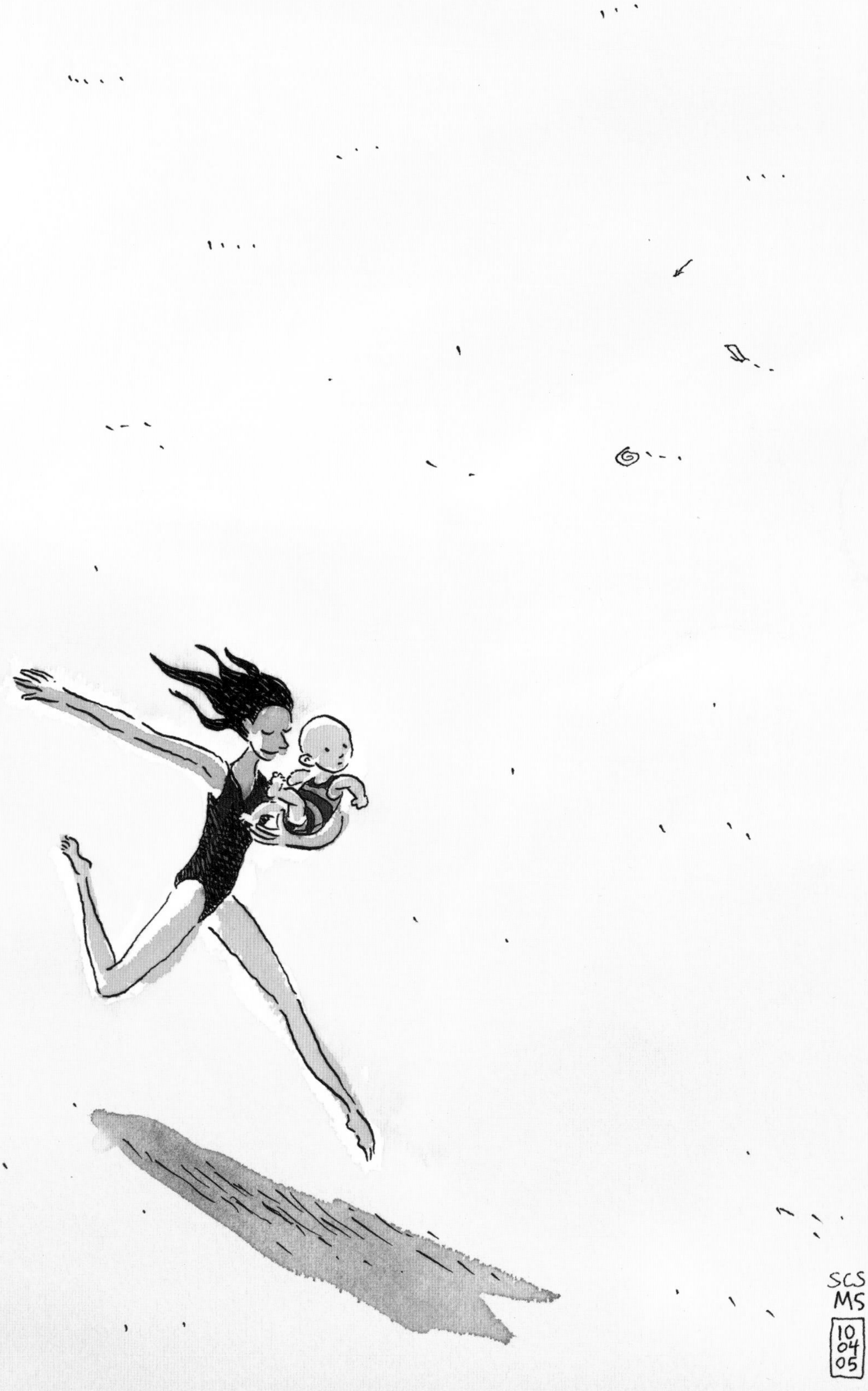
SCS
MS
10
04
05